THE CURSE OF SEAL VALLEY

The storm had defeated her.

Sula clung to a floating raft of planks, left her by the destroying waves, clung without knowing she clung, clung to life, longing for life and for calm seas and quiet waters and land beneath her feet.

She was carried past the oil rig and taken by the oil.

She was dark with oil, a seal woman, dark face and dark hair, and body slimed with blackness. The seal pup drifted close to her, knocked against her, and she heard its shrill whimper of fear born of exhaustion and panic. She held its cold flipper, clinging to it, because the seal pup, like her, was alive and alone in the wild maelstrom of boiling water and drifting oil . . .

The Curse of Seal Valley

Joyce Stranger

CAROUSEL BOOKS
A DIVISION OF TRANSWORLD PUBLISHERS LTD.

THE CURSE OF SEAL VALLEY

A CAROUSEL BOOK 0 552 52207 4

First publication in Great Britain by J.M. Dent & Sons
Limited

PRINTING HISTORY

J.M. Dent & Sons Limited edition published 1979
Carousel edition published 1982

Carousel Books are published by
Transworld Publishers Ltd.,
Century House, 61–63 Uxbridge Road,
Ealing, London W5 5SA

Made and printed in Great Britain by
Cox & Wyman Ltd., Reading.

At Carreg Castle, which is a ruin near Llandeilo, in Wales, there is a tunnel 150 feet long which is the entrance to a wishing well that was once very famous.

To make a wish come true, corks and pins were thrown into the water, which had healing powers.

At Llaneilian-yn-Rhos, near Colwyn Bay there is a cursing well. Those who wished to destroy an enemy paid the keeper who wrote their names on a piece of paper. This was wrapped round a stone and dropped into the water. People had to pay to have their names removed as the curse lasted while the paper was in the well. It functioned until 1929 when it was covered, but the local people all know where it is, and rumour says it can still be used.

In Loch Duich, in Ross and Cromarty the seals played at night. They could shed their skins when they wished and one night three brothers stole three seal skins belonging to three lovely seal girls. These the brothers took as wives. The youngest pitied his who mourned for her family and let her go. But she had fallen in love and was allowed to visit him once every nine nights.

Terrible troubles came to the other two brothers who had held their wives by force.

There is also the story of the girl who fell in love with a seal man and had a child.

And a whole clan in North Uist who are descended from such a marriage.

1

The wind that savaged the beaches was a death wind from hell. It thrust the sea against the rocks that leaped out of the foaming water; it flung the sea against the cliffs that crumbled under its onslaught. It dragged weed and shingle in a wicked undertow that tore everything in its path away from its moorings and tossed it into the seething waves.

The bull seals had left the shore, to ride the storm in the deep waters. The cows were marooned by the needs of their babies; helpless, almost newborn, flung up and down the beaches like driftwood, torn away from their grieving mothers who tried, vainly, to interpose their own bodies between the pups and the grasping water that crashed and thundered around them.

The bull pup at the edge of the tide was older than the rest. He had been born nearly half a moon before; he had strength but not enough strength. He had knowledge of calm days and soothing waters on which he rode, rocking gently, playing at his mother's side; diving and surfacing, basking in the sun, scratching an itch with a lazy flipper.

His world had been a good world until the demons of the dark came striding out of the night, flinging unseen pebbles at him; shrieking in his ears. The noise of surf and thunder, of rock holding fast against the onslaught of the tide, whipped by a frenzied wind, the sweep and

7

suck of shingle, was deafening; beyond it sounded the cries of terrified sea birds, mewing and calling as water invaded their nesting sites and tore their eggs from beneath them and took the new hatched young. Added to the din was the baying of the mother seals, crying to their young, crying for their young, crying for the pups that were tossed on the water and flung helplessly against the wicked rocks that had seen the end of many a good boat as well as many a defenceless seal baby.

The bull pup had been lying at his mother's side, when the sea took him. He tried to swim, but the over-powering strength of the waves and the cruel surf drove him back to the land, flinging him carelessly, tossing him again and again on the boulders, only to suck him back again, toying with him as a cat toys with the shrew she has caught but will never eat because she knows it is poison. Yet still she teases and kills.

He could not fight the powers of the crashing waves.

Slowly, remorselessly, the sea drew him away from the land, out on to the deep. All around him was darkness.

Darkness.

A swirling mist.

And the sea birds crying.

The green waves crashing.

Death in the sea and death on the rocks and death in the creeping ooze that festered and seethed where the oil slick crept on the yellow sands; where the oil slick lay on the rippled pools; where the dark oil covered the living rocks.

The seagulls were caught and slimed.

The shellfish died.

The fish gasped for life, and life forsook them.

Nothing survived.

Only the seal baby drifted, half alive, knowing nothing; life within him keeping a brave hold.

All around him was the surging sea, the great waves that spattered the slick and broke it; and then, as the breakers crashed, held it and flung it wide and far. He lifted his head, but there was oil in his eyes and he saw nothing. He was aware of life near him.

Of a presence beside him.

Of another living creature, though he knew nothing about that creature. It moved against him, groped for his flipper; gave him the courage to fight against darkness and the choking air, and the swiftly surging relentless sea and the needled rocks that tore and scratched and bruised him.

Her name was Sula.

She lived in a country torn by war. Men came out of the night with guns and bombs and killed. They killed her mother, her father and her baby brother.

Sula hid.

She hid in the dark garden and slipped into the night. The men who had come to destroy her family thought she had died with them, for they set fire to the house.

They did not look for her.

She lived for weeks on roots and berries and slept under the trees. She travelled in the darkness until she came to the sea.

The sea tossed in front of her.

There was freedom across the water in a land where no one threw bombs; or not very often. Not like her land.

She heard mens' voices, and ran along the shore.

The boat that lay there was old and it had no oars, but as the voices came nearer and the gunshots sounded, the need to escape outweighted everything else.

She pushed the boat into the sea.

She let it drift with the current and drift with the waves.

She had no food and no water.

She had only hope.

Hope of sanctuary, far away from her homeland where no one would find her. She had nobody left. A new world; a new life; a new beginning; if she reached another shore.

She had never been to sea before.

She feared the wind.

She feared the great waves.

She lay in the bottom of the boat, not caring whether she lived or died. Out of the sky came a wind greater than any she had known before that took the boat and tossed it high, that took the boat and flung it down the long sliding sides of enormous green breakers, that filled it with white water.

There was only wind and water and the roaring from the sky.

Clouds, so full of rain that they almost touched the water, broke, and soaked her. She had never known such misery.

Almost, she wished she had died with her family.

But life is strong, and she fought without knowing she fought.

She watched the clouds part and the sun shine and the clouds spread again.

She watched the sea quieten, but then the storm came back from a different direction.

She saw the lights of an oil rig but she did not know what they were.

She saw the darkness spreading on the water.

Oil for riches.

Oil for death.

She was thirsty beyond any thirst that she had ever known. She was hungry beyond any hunger that she had ever known.

She was so tired that she did not think she would ever wake again if she fell asleep.

She saw the white wings of the wheeling gulls as they flew above her.

She saw the sun die in the waters and the moon ride the sky.

She heard the breakers crashing on a distant shore.

She had no strength left. She prayed.

The boat hit a rock; before she realized what had happened it had sunk but she was floating on the wild sea.

There was no one near to help.

She did not know what shore waited there; were they the cliffs of her homeland and were all her terrors endured in vain? Or were they the cliffs of a land that promised sanctuary?

The storm had defeated her.

She clung to a floating raft of planks, left her by the destroying waves, clung without knowing she clung, clung to life, longing for life and for calm seas and quiet waters and land beneath her feet.

She was carried past the oil rig and taken by the oil.

She had forgotten day.

There was only darkness and the surge and suck and spray of the green waters.

She was dark with oil, a seal woman, dark face and dark hair, and body slimed with blackness. The seal pup drifted close to her, knocked against her, and she heard its shrill whimper of fear born of exhaustion and panic. She held its cold flipper, clinging to it, because the seal pup, like her, was alive and alone in the wild maelstrom of boiling water and drifting oil.

The seal pup drew comfort from a living creature, holding on to it, reassuring it. It had never known humans and had no fear.

11

They floated on.

They were almost beyond hope, almost beyond help.

The seas pounded them. The girl clung to the raft and clung to the seal but her strength was dying.

Night came once more.

Black clouds were torn from the face of the moon.

Golden light shone on the desecrated beach and mocked the spoiled sand.

2

Hugh lived alone at the head of the haunted valley.
Few people came to the valley; only those whose hatred
bore them on charmed feet towards the Cursing Well
beyond Hugh's hut.

Here they wrote the names of their enemies on
minute paper flags, which they pinned, banner like,
on to a cork, and tossed them into the stagnant waters,
with the words that had come down in time from the
Ancients.

> Curse thee living,
> Curse thee dead,
> Curse thy meat,
> Curse thy bread,
> Curse thee morning,
> Curse thee night,
> Deep and sorry,
> Be thy plight.

Those who came there and saw the tall man, half
hidden among the bushes, watching them from under
eyebrows that bristled above deep grey eyes, thought
that he was the guardian of the well, living there to
help implement their curses.

They did not know that, when they had gone, he
took a stick with a hooked wire on the end and drew the
little craft of evil towards him. Then, taking the name

13

and the pin from the cork, he sprinkled the paper with holy water from the charmed place at Glastonbury, marking above in ink the sign of the cross, to remove all evil.

That done, he restored the bobbing cork to the water. Few ever knew that their curse had failed, for most forgot their enmity, and others were ashamed. For all that, the wiser folk in the village avoided the well, which had a long history of misery behind it.

No one drank from it.

Long ago, the old houses that were now ruins had been prosperous, surrounding the well, but then came the Plague that raced headlong over Britain. The village was isolated and the people died. The houses crumbled into ruins and windflower and bindweed, thistle, nettle and dock took over. Jays nested in the tall trees, and screamed in warning, sounding like the repeated wails of the long ago dying. A new village was built, farther away from the valley.

When Hugh left the sea, he had a wife and a small son. One day, the car his wife was driving was hit by a runaway lorry when its brakes failed. His wife and son both died.

When all was done, he left his home, taking only a few possessions to the hut in the woods, built long ago for a shepherd guarding his flock. He did not want folk around him. He did not want to see children running to school.

He made his life in the woods, among the animals, trapping what he needed, but rarely eating meat. He grew his own vegetables; he harvested young nettles for soup and dandelion leaves for salad. He fed the deer in winter, and the forest ponies came to him as if he were their master.

He took the oiled gulls from the beaches, cleaned them and nursed them back to health. There was a small pond beside the hut where pure, fresh water came from a bubbling stream. Here he kept his first seal, which had been washed out to sea and was a victim of an earlier oil leak. Mostly the small beast lived out of the water, but each day followed Hugh down the cliff path to the sands where he swam in the breakers.

They were washed ashore together, the woman and the seal baby, lying side by side on the sands. Black oil disfigured them both.

Oil for riches.

Oil for death.

The slick had been reported two days before, ten miles long and many yards wide, pouring from an oil rig already damaged by a previous gale. The aftermath of the gale lay, telltale, on the smothered sands. Gobs of oil, branches of trees, and the debris of civilization, from plastic strips of dirty sheeting to plastic cups and food wrappings, lying where once only seaweed, rotting in the sun, had marred the damp sand.

When day was bright, Hugh saw the seal and saw the woman. He hurried to find out if they were still alive. The woman was so oil covered she was barely human. The seal had moved and she had not.

Now the baby seal in the pool beside his cottage would have a companion. Hugh had locked him in the hut when he heard about the oil slick. It had taken days to clean the animal and weeks to remedy the damage done to him by the oil that had clogged mouth and eyes and ears and nose, and lodged inside him. Hugh did not want further trouble.

The seal baby tried to turn to its side, and the shape beside it moved too, twisting its head away from the sand, trying to lift it from the ground. Hugh knelt, looked closer, and saw deep brown eyes, filled with tears, staring at him from a face that was

15

unrecognizable as male or female. But the oil soaked hair must surely be that of a woman for it grew waist long, part of the sticky strands lying across the seal.

Hugh lifted the struggling figure. It was a woman, perhaps only a girl, whose fingers clutched at him. He assisted her to her feet, the oil from her smothering him too, and he helped her, lagging, slow by slow step, through the sand that gripped their feet, along the beach and up the steps. Twice he looked back.

The oily tide was turning, slipping back to low. The seal baby would still be there when he returned.

Though it might not be alive.

He brought a wooden chair out of the hut and covered it with grass cuttings. He sat the girl down, and brought cotton waste and soapy water and tried to clean her face. He worked slowly, carefully, and after a few minutes the girl took some of the waste and tried to clean her hands.

He went indoors, to heat up broth for her. He wondered how she had come to be in the sea.

When he returned she spoke to him, in a soft lilting voice that used words that meant nothing to him. He had never heard her language before.

He was used to talking to animals; teaching them to understand him and trying to understand them. He knew the warning clarion gongcall of the cock pheasant and started to alertness himself when it sounded. He knew the angry clap of pigeon wings as a stranger came near; he knew the talk of eyes. The brown eyes that looked at him now were afraid; afraid of him, the oil that clung to her and of this strange land where the man spoke in a tongue she had never heard.

But she understood the bowl and the hot soup, and she sipped it gratefully, and the shivering stopped.

Hugh brought the little seal from the hut. He had called the beast Toma, and he spoke its name now. He pointed to the oil on her and to Toma, twice, and she understood and nodded. There was no sign of oil now on the little creature; he frisked happily on the grass in front of her, his doglike head turning to look at this stranger who had come to his home.

Hugh pointed to the beach, and to the seal and the girl understood. She had seen the seal beside her; perhaps they had been together before they were caught by the slick. He did not know.

He brought her cleaning cloths and more warm soapy water; a special soap that he made himself. The girl nodded her thanks, and pointed to the beach.

Hugh went, back past the well, where he saw another curse craft bobbing. He must remember to change the curse to a blessing. Someone had been up there while he was away.

The seal baby had struggled a little way along the beach. It was bewildered and felt ill and yet hungry, and its mother had vanished.

Hugh was conscious of its fear as he lifted the animal.

The oil was slippery and the seal was hard to hold.

He looked at the smothered beach.

It would be weeks before it was clean again and daily he must come to seek for other creatures, so that he could help them.

Some would die.

Oil for riches.

Oil for death.

He hated oil.

As he struggled up the slope he toyed with the idea of writing the word oil on a cursing flag, and putting the pin on the cork and consigning it to the water. He mocked himself, laughing at the sky, that was clean with wind and clouds, clear with sunlight, free for the soaring birds.

A kestrel hovered above him, on the wind.

He toiled up the steps. The seal baby was heavy.

He paused at the top.

The hut door was open. Smoke plumed from the chimney. Toma came to greet him, with his ungainly flapping walk that turned to streamlined grace when he was in the water. The girl came out of the doorway. She had not yet cleaned all the oil, but her face was almost clear, and the long black hair clung wetly against her, like a sealskin.

Hugh remembered the old stories of the seal women who came from the sea. They changed at night to seals and by day to human women. She had come from nowhere, out of the sea, speaking a tongue that he had never heard.

Toma went to her, lifting his head to greet her and she bent, and rubbed noses with him and laughed.

Hugh stared at her.

He had rescued a seal woman, and he would keep her for ever. He would marry her and they would have sons, to replace the son he had lost. But would his sons be seals?

He was not an imaginative man, but the old legends had been told him at the fireside by his grandmother, and they returned in force. The songs of the seal women longing to return to their ocean homes, and the songs of the men who were left alone.

One day, would she return to the sea? Or did she belong already to some other man?

She moved towards him, smiling up at him and lifted the oil-covered baby from his arms, and knelt, laying it on the grass, taking the cotton waste to clean eyes and nose and nostrils, crooning to it softly as mothers all over the world crooned to their young.

The kestrel was gone.

The wind freshened.

Hugh watched the girl work and the sense of alone-
ness that had been his for so many years, eased and
vanished. If only she would stay . . . he looked at the
hut and the glen and the pool; he had so little. Was she
a sea king's bride, from a palace under the waves? Or
was she some shipwrecked princess, from a country
over the sea? Or was she a rich man's daughter, swept
overboard from his yacht?

She could not tell him yet, but perhaps, one day, if
she stayed, she would learn his language and he would
discover the truth.

Meanwhile, there was much to do.

3

Gwyn grew up in the village but was never part of the village. His mother lived in a small hut at the top of the cliffs, where the wind flung itself against the rock and the sea surged in fury. He grew up with a darkness in his head; a darkness made up of frequent anger with a world that was never kind.

His mother knitted for the villagers. She was never clean; her grey hair flew on the wild wind and her grey clothes flew behind her too, so that when she walked, there was a weird whirling around her, that frightened the children.

They feared Gwyn when he was angry.

He was wild and rough and had only one asset. He had a beautiful voice that sang strange songs at night time, walking the cliffs, singing to the sea. And he learned to tell wild lies. He told of maidens with long shining hair and shining fish tails who walked on the beaches in the darkness and danced on the sands singing to him. Sometimes he sang their songs.

He told of a wild white horse that came from the sea and cantered along the beach and how he had tamed it; it came only for him.

The children laughed at his stories.

Gwyn the Lie, they called him.

One day, they would believe him.

One day, they would learn to value the tales he told.

One day, he would be the most important man in all the village; more important than the minister at the chapel; more important than the vicar.

More important than Dai the Police, or Maldwyn the Farm, or even than Evans the Post, who knew everything that happened in the village before it happened.

Gwyn's mother died.

There was no more money from knitting, so that Gwyn went to the beach, to find what he could and to live how he could. He found cockles and winkles and put them in sacks and hawked them round the houses and the women bought from him because they were afraid of his wild tongue if they refused him.

He sold seaweed to the farmers to put on their land.

He caught shrimps with his net, and sold them to the village wives. Sometimes he borrowed a boat, not asking if he might, for Gwyn asked favours of no one and took what he wanted if it were left around, and he caught fish and sold them too to the village.

He lived, after a fashion.

His hut held little but his colour television set. Always, whatever else he did, he paid the rent for the wonderful box that showed him the beautiful houses where rich people lived. One day he would have such a house; a house with big rooms and beautiful furniture and curtains that hung from the ceiling to the floor. A proper house that had several levels and a gallery, with plants in pots that made the place look as if there were a garden indoors.

He dreamed at nights of such a house.

Sometimes he woke, and was angry because he was still in his hut and the television set was a dead thing, that showed no pictures. Then he walked on the cliffs, and sang to the moon and his singing was heard by those who came home late, and they hurried, lest

Gwyn catch up with them. They were never sure that his anger would end with words.

The singing resounded on quiet nights, the tune beating out with the words that hurled themselves into the air. Gwyn made up the words; they were often angry and told of his longing and his needs for riches and for his wonderful house, and for his garden inside the house. They were words that defied the people around him, daring them to harm him; words that spoke of his white horse that came from the sea and how he mastered it and rode it across the world at night, and it stamping with its raging hooves on those that maddened him.

It was a wild horse; a man's horse; a raging stallion, powered as was Gwyn, by hate of the real world that would not let him share its wealth. He looked in at the night-bright windows and saw the children with their mothers, saw the warm fires and the tables laid with food; saw the babies cuddled close.

No one had ever cuddled him close.

His mother had pushed him away, and told him to go and play outside. She had to knit to provide for both of them.

'If I was alone,' she'd say, and look at him from black fierce eyes that seemed to him to hate him, as if he did not belong in her life; as if he had come as an intruder, unwanted, and half feared.

He would lie in his narrow bed at night and listen to her talking to herself. Sometimes she frightened him. Sometimes she worried him; always she pushed him away from her.

He had sat at a school desk but learning had had no meaning. Words would not make sense when they were letters on a page; figures meant nothing written down in black on white paper. He had loved the stories they told him; tales of knights in armour, of ruthless men who fought and killed. He had learned to write in his own way — words spelled as they sounded.

One day he would conquer the whole world; he would show he was master. Men would fear him. Men would bow down in front of him as they bowed to the ancient gods.

He learned to curse and his curses were always on the water.

He learned to live free and to live rough and to make men hate him.

He ran through the full moon nights, shouting to the sea to come and fight him, and flung himself into the roaring waves and challenged them, struggling against them, swimming more like a seal than a man.

He jumped on the cliffs, daring the night to overwhelm him with darkness and he sang to the moon, a hound baying its need, yet never knowing what it needed.

Those who heard him said their prayers and huddled under the bedclothes.

He loved the striding wind that fought the trees. It shouted to him, filling him with excitement so that he felt his power. Power over all men; power over words; power that soon they would recognize.

As he grew older so his thoughts grew wilder.

He shook his fists at the children.

They ran.

Gwyn laughed and the laughter echoed against the cliffs like thunder.

He shook his fists at the cattle and the sheep; at the men who passed him. He longed to meet them and talk to them and convert them to liking him, but he did not know how. So he would make them fear him.

One day he would meet them; they would listen to him. He would learn the secrets that everyone else knew. They would obey him, and then he would make them do as he wished. He would make Dafydd the House build him a great house, and Evans the Post would bring him letters — letters full of money. Mair the shop would give him her goods free; cheese and bacon and butter and eggs. Angharad the pigs would make him a warm jersey to wear in winter when the frost hung on the bushes, and the world was white-coated, and the grass crunched under his feet.

Ayeee, it was cold on those winter days and his little hut had only a little fire and that made from wood gathered on the beach. No money for coals for warmth and no money for logs from Gareth the Trees.

He hated Hugh, because Hugh had skills that men honoured and he was the keeper of the Cursing Well.

Unlike Gwyn the daftie from up on the cliffs who all men laughed at behind his back; Gwyn the Lie, with his tall stories; Gwyn the savage with his wild temper and you never knew when one of those was coming on.

It was better to make sure Hugh was fed; and to avoid Gwyn except to buy from him, lest he smashed the flowers in your garden and threw bad fish through your open windows.

That year, there was wind all the time; and with the wind Gwyn grew in power and grew in madness.

But that, no one knew.

They thought him a little twisted in the head; not quite the same as they were, but they could not see the eating terror that darkened his brain and made him a man to be feared and avoided; and never a man to be mocked at.

He knew they mocked when he was gone; he crept back, silent as a night-time prowling cat, and listened.

He did not like the things they said.

He waited.

His time would come.

And when the moon was high and full again, he sang

his songs of hate across the cliff tops and knew that he rode his wild stallion, high in the sky, among the clouds and its powerful hooves trod down the little men, far below him, who angered him so.

4

The village was isolated by water and by mountains. The wide river cut it off from the town; it was miles to the road bridge. The high hills soared above it, sometimes shadowed by sombre cloud; sometimes lightened by rays of sun; always changing, but there for eternity, giving shelter to the wild mountain sheep and the eagles and the goats that lived their lives remote from man on the steep plateaus where only the solitary climbers came to challenge the rocks, and test their skills against the unyielding gods of the dark ranges.

It was easy for the villagers to believe the old stories; the demons of darkness often rumbled their rage across the mountain tops and the children were told stories of the Lady who came from the lake, bringing her cattle with her. She married a village man, who was told he must never strike her. But he did; not in anger, but once in fun and once in sorrow, and once when she swallowed an apple pip and almost choked.

She left him; and she left him three fine sons. At midnight every Midsummer Eve she came from the lake and her husband watched her from afar, not able to come near lest she vanish; but she spoke to her sons and taught them the lore of healing. She taught the virtues of the herbs that grew on the high hills to Rhiwallon, her eldest son, and he taught in turn to his own three sons, Cadwgan, Gruffyd and Einion, who, long ago when the world was much younger, were the physicians of the Myddfai.

Hugh, so his father said, traced his ancestry back to them. His father taught him the art of healing with herbs, but he did not practise it, for the villagers were afraid of him; of his long hair and beard and his eyes, haunted by sorrow for the wife and child he had lost. He did not wish to speak with other men, and he avoided women.

He grew herbs in his garden; rosemary, rue and lavender; fennel, dandelion and dock; mint, parsley and thyme; camomile, catnip and valerian. Sometimes, when he heard folk talking, of a child or a woman that was sick, he would make a brew and take it and leave it on the doorstep. And later see the victim walking well again, and know that his simples had cured the ill.

Those he healed were his friends, and brought food to the hidden valley, leaving him cheese, eggs, pastries, bread and cakes. Some of them hoped to stave off the evil they thought he might bring to the village. Those he had cured brought him thanks, knowing him a good man, no matter what rumour said.

But there were always those who believed ill of everyone.

The worst of these was Gwyn.

His curse crafts were always on the haunted water.

Gwyn cursed the farmer where he worked, for upbraiding him when he lost his temper with a cow, and hit her with his closed fist. He cursed the baker who would not sell him a loaf of bread for half its price; he cursed the girl who refused to marry him.

His curses never came to pass, as always Hugh watched for the little cork crafts that carried such venom, and took them and blessed them. The farmer prospered and the baker became esteemed for his bread all over the village; and the girl married and had three fine sons.

Gwyn grew morose and even more wicked tempered. The children learned to run when they saw him striding down the street, his stick swinging in his hands, ready to lash out at dog or cat or child that crossed his path.

Gwyn was on the cliff top when the woman and the seal baby were tossed up by the tide.

He hated Hugh, and he feared him, for more than once he had met the man and crossed words with him. Hugh, patient and gentle, refused to be angered and, believing solidly in the faith of the Christian and the power of goodness, made Gwyn always feel as if he had lost a battle that he did not know he was fighting.

Also his curses always misfired and he was sure that Hugh had some greater magic than he, for his mother had taught him the use of many strange plants, not to heal, but to bewilder and to be-devil.

Gwyn watched Hugh help the girl up the beach; saw her seal-like coat of oil. He had the hermit in his power. Here was proof of evil indeed, for here was a seal woman changed to human form, with her baby beside her. As yet, the seal baby showed no sign of human shape, but perhaps his powers would grow. Here, indeed, was devilry.

That night, talking in the inn, he told of what he had seen.

The men were bored; life was dull; they listened.

He loved to talk, and when he drank words came easily, plausibly, quickly, until he believed his lies were true and made other men believe him.

The men eyed one another uneasily. Old Mr Evans from the small holding beyond the river, laughed at such superstition, but he came from the mainland, where men were unbelieving. Those who lived in the

28

village knew that strange things could happen; had happened in the past and would happen again, for the margin between man and animal was small. There were wolves that howled in the mountains by night where no wolf should be; and men with wild eyes who came down in the morning from the howling places. There were birds that had men's eyes, and watched inimically and cawed their curses. There were girls who fled from those who would harm them and turned into deer, vanishing as if they had never been, while the police came and asked foolish questions, not knowing that here the unbelievable came to pass and the mundane rational reason was always a lie.

There were those too who knew of another well and a secret tunnel that led to it. Those who were good beyond average found the tunnel, and crept through the rock, and came out into a valley where the sun always shone and flowers always bloomed, and deer and rabbits and hares were tame to the hand. The bright birds sang and sunshine sparkled on leaping water and the favoured were free to wish, so long as the wish was never a selfish wish but for the good of others.

There were few who found the way; Hugh had found it, soon after his wife died. He wished for nothing, for there was no one left for whom he wanted favours, but sometimes, when his heart was too heavy to bear existence he crept back through the twisting rock, and came into the little glade. Lying by the water, and watching bird and beast he came back whole again.

Here, once, he had picked some elder flowers, more beautiful than those in the valley where he lived. He planted the bush, then plucked the leaves and brewed a bath for Sula, to ease her sore skin. He told her it was called Bedydd Ceridwen, or Ceridwen's Baptism, for it was first used in the magic cauldron of Ceridwen herself. The Welsh girls who bathed in it spat three times

29

into the water, but it was too difficult to describe this to Sula, who knew nothing of English or of Welsh. The water soothed and eased her.

Gwyn saw Hugh prepare the bath. Here was more magic; more wickedness, for Gwyn knew only of evil through herbs and not of healing. His mother and his grandmother had known only wickedness and passed it on.

There was rarely work for Gwyn in the village now. His hands were cursed; everything he touched stuck to them, so that money and food vanished when Gwyn worked there; and sometimes other things vanished too. His head was cursed for he had an angry tongue and saw insult in every word that others spoke.

His legs now were cursed too, for they ached day and night and he was twisted outside as well as in. He ran, bent kneed, sidelong, crabwise, frightening the children even more so that their mothers did not need to invent bogey men to take them away, for, if they were bad then Gwyn would come for them and make faces at them. His day by day face was ugly enough but his angry face was enough to frighten the ravens off their nests. Only in the water could he move with ease.

Winter came. There was snow on the ground, but Hugh had built his hut snugly, and though Sula spoke little of his tongue, on one fine morning he took her to the minister and they were wed. And with them, wherever they went, were the two little seals, flapping after them down to the beach, coming to them for food, rubbing against Sula who always greeted them with her nose, putting her head down to them as their mothers once had done, knowing they were lonely for the mothers they had lost and trying to give them security and affection.

At first the village had laughed at Gwyn.

But now they began to wonder, for daily Sula ran down to the sea with the seal pups behind her, and together they swam in the waves. When her long dark hair was slick and wet and close against her head, then there were three dark seal heads on the water. Hugh watched them, laughing at their antics, admiring the way his new wife swam, enjoying every moment of her company. He took her to the wishing well; she too was blessed and accepted and the way was clear for them, and there, he knew, she had wished, but he did not know her wish. He only knew that with her coming, the bitterness had eased, and perhaps one day he would have a son again.

Meantime he had a wife and they had Toma and Tonto to cheer them. Tonto earned his name by the strange noise he made to call them when he was hungry.

Hugh fished for them all.

Sula kept the hut clean and bought material for curtains and covers and proved to embroider like an angel. Her quick fingers made endless patterns of flowers and birds.

One day Hugh brought her new linen and new silks; and she began to embroider the healing plants for him. Elder flower and a maiden bathing; cowslip flowers, and a woman sleeping; the pictures grew, and she left the cloth by the hut one morning and Gwyn saw it, and knew that here was yet more witchcraft, for was she not making pictures of the villagers, and of the herbs that would cripple or make idiot, or kill?

Again he told the old men in the inn at night.

The men did not trust him; and yet they looked at one another and said wisely that there was never smoke without fire. And the woman had come from the sea, from nowhere, and she spoke no language that any man ever knew, and she had the two seal babies and

31

surely that was all the proof they needed?

Gwyn made a plan, but he needed time.

He hated Hugh with a hatred that grew daily when he saw that the man was looking younger; his long grey hair, neatly cut, appeared darker than before; his beard, neatly trimmed, gave him a handsome look that had been lacking. He moved with the step of a young man again; he laughed again; he played with the seal babies and treasured his young wife, making her a bower to rest in when the sun was hot, growing her flowers to tell her the things that he could not tell her for he did not know the words in her tongue. He grew broom for faithfulness; and blue Canterbury bells for devotion; and buttercup for radiance; picking the flowers and holding them against her chin to see the yellow shine there.

Gwyn watched from his hidden eyrie, secret as a deer in a thicket, planning and hating. Envy made him even uglier than before and though the old men now listened to him and some of the younger men, the women avoided him and the children feared him, sensing in him the wickedness that was worse than anything their elders could imagine or believe.

Gwyn hated the children, knowing that their eyes saw clearly, and that they would never trust nor believe him, as their grandfathers did.

Hatred mastered him, and envy, for Hugh laughed and the seal woman played with the pups and swam in the water, and everything flourished around them. At night Gwyn went back to a desolate cottage, the roof and walls in need of repair, the paper peeling off with damp, the floors unscrubbed and filthy with the dirt of years.

He went, briefly, to help with the pigs at the farm that nestled in the trees under the Great Mountain. Clouds soared above the high peaks and the wind cried for ever, sometimes in a soft whining that sent the new-born rabbit and hare babies scurrying for shelter, afraid of this invisible beast that whimpered in the grasses. Sometimes it moaned so that the marauding fox, who was braver than any beast on the mountain and far more cunning, was scared. Sometimes, in a high scream of fury, the wind raced along the mountain flank, tearing tiles and slates from roof tops, bending the trees to its will until they too screamed for mercy, sometimes tossing an ageing giant from the ground to lie with roots exposed to the sky, avoided alike by running fox and wild pony and hidden deer.

The wind always moaned round the farmyard, echoing Gwyn's bitter mood. He fed and cleaned the pigs and he hated them. Pigs were the mainstay of the village and nowhere else in Wales did they come so fine and fat. Men came from miles around to buy them for market and the wealth of the village was in the pigs.

Gryfydd Evans was one of the best farmers in the village. He loved his pigs, and had nothing else to love, for his children were grown and married and lived overseas and his wife had died ten years before. He was an old man now, his face creased with long living, but merry, his eyes lit by laughter. He had names for his sows and he loved nothing more than to walk with a feeding bottle under one arm and give milk to a busy sucking little animal that tugged and fought to feed, and butted him in anger when the milk did not come fast enough or had gone. He did not like Gwyn but he had hurt his back and there was no one else to help him.

Gwyn worked slowly; he never worked well; he left muck in the corners of the styes and forgot fresh water. He gave mouldy swill to Titanic, the big boar who was too wise to eat it and called his rage all day until Gryff went to see what ailed him, and found the telltale uneaten food in the corner of the stye.

Once more Gwyn was without a job; and this time his ears were ringing with angry words and bitter reprimands, of which the least was 'useless' and the worst he could remember until the day he died for Gryff had an eloquent tongue and preached in chapel on Sundays, to the consternation of wrong doers, who quivered under the lash of his words.

Gwyn made a curse upon Gryff and his pigs.

This time he would make it good and he would make it true and he would ensure that it came to pass.

He went out at midnight when the moon was full to look for rue, gall and wormwood; for witchbane, dreadwort, devil's bit and the little rare white eye that pigs hated; for every plant his mother had ever shown him, and her mother before her, to wreak evil.

But he did not make the brew to give to the pigs, as that way, he would be caught. This time he would be subtle and outwit them all.

He made the brew, and when the moon was again at the full he took his brew to the Devil's Stone, and there, with a goosefeather, he wrote his curse on a piece of slate. It was the best curse that he had ever invented and he had invented many. He cursed Gryff, and his pigs. He cursed Hugh and Sula. He cursed the villagers. All of them.

This curse would not float.

It would sink, deep into the evil depths of the cursing well; out of sight of any man, to work its cunning over the months. It would be slow work; devil's work.

That night, when Hugh and Sula slept, Gwyn crept over the tussocky grass, softly, breathlessly, his scent masked by the skins of new killed rabbits. The seal pups smelled the blood and were afraid but they did not smell man.

The collie cur that slept at Hugh's side on the mat

34

beside the bed lifted a lip, but did not smell man.

Gwyn crept to the edge of the water.

The well was deep and dark and surrounded by strange plants that grew nowhere else. The moon hung above the water yet there was no reflection.

He slipped his hand into the water, and let the slate fall.

Let the curse be fulfilled.

Let the village rot.

Let all men suffer as I am suffering.

Let no one survive.

Let all happiness leave the place.

He smiled crookedly to himself as he walked home. No one would find his curse or turn his curse to good, as he now believed that Hugh had changed the words on many a curse craft. Hugh would never find the slate.

The words, made with secret ink, made with witchcraft, made with ill wishing and with moon luck and the luck of the Devil's Stone, could never be erased.

He ran, swiftly sidling, shouting his songs at the sky; shouting his hate of the world and his curse rhymes, in his strange sweet voice that did not seem to belong to him at all.

And he called to the sky to his wild horse, his stallion, to come from the clouds and carry him to the hills and trample his enemies; he called it to him, longing for vengeance and when it came he rode it and his songs grew jubilant, and he knew such power as few men dreamed of.

A waking boy heard the singing, and being daring he looked from the window of his room.

The moon shone on the cliff tops.

The boy saw no horse.

He only saw Gwyn, capering and yelling, his voice flung back from the rocks, standing above the sea, staring out at the path swathed across it flung by the moon.

35

He saw Gwyn turn and run away, his hands held before him as if he rode a horse; his body moving up and down as if there were a horse beneath him. Yet his legs moved like a man's legs, twisted and betraying him and the boy saw, not the wild gallop, but the clumsy movements of Gwyn the Lie, Gwyn the Fool, Gwyn the man to be feared and avoided.

Had he dared, he would have laughed.

But his sister who was older than he and so wiser, said that Gwyn's strange powers, witch powers, had been inherited from his mother, the cobweb woman who had strode through the village with her wild grey hair and her wild grey clothes. She had brought wicked magic so that the cows sickened when she had been by, and the pigs had swine fever, and the children suffered from terrible boils.

Better not to risk such troubles.

Better to sleep and forget the man who ran through the night, singing to the sky.

The boy drew the covers over his head to keep out the demons of the night.

Beyond the cove Gwyn sang on, and knew that his wild horse pranced under him and that one day soon they would ride the night wind and rule the world and all men would tremble when he passed.

He stood there, laughing.

Ho, ho, ho, ho, ho.

The laughter echoed and the sea birds huddled closer, fearing the terrible sounds.

5

Sula had her new life. It was as if her old life had never existed. Sometimes, sitting quietly in the doorway of the home that Hugh had rebuilt for her, she thought back to the land in which she had been born; to the long winter snows and the frozen rivers. There were the men singing songs in the cold dark evenings; and her mother, braiding her hair, and her baby brother and father. All now dead.

She could not tell Hugh yet where she came from, for her name for her own country was a strange one, in her own tongue. She had come from the sea and Hugh was happy and she belonged to him. That was enough. She never wanted to go back to a country ruled by anger and fear — by men who spoke through their guns and killed casually.

Sometimes, in the winter, her fingers embroidered strange scenes; men in furs fishing through ice holes; seals on ice floes and a polar bear. Hugh knew the animals and told her the name for them. She was learning his tongue, though it was not easy. She had visited the ice country. She did not want to remember her own country. It reminded her of anguish and loss. Better to embroider her dreams and memories of a time that was good when they were altogether, enjoying a holiday in a new land, far from her own home. They had travelled overland for many days.

The seal pups came into the house and lay in their pen in the corner, close against one another. They were growing big now. Hugh thought perhaps, when summer came, the pups would return to the sea, being old enough to look after themselves.

They had taught them to catch the fish that abounded in the shallow water. They were bonny and strong, and they were as much fun as the dogs, each with endearing ways. Tomas was bold and over curious; it was Tomas who burnt his nose on the hot kettle; and Tomas who almost overturned the oil lamp; and it was Tomas who floundered into the bog and had to be rescued. Tonto was cautious, sniffing his way about the place; wary of heat and wary of cold, wary, at first of water, perhaps remembering the wildness that had tossed him helpless into the sea.

There was a pool for them now, as well as the wide beach, so that they could swim near to home when they wished.

Hugh was making a garden. He had almost reached the Cursing Well, but this defeated him for no matter how often he weeded the ground around it, the wild flowers came back; such flowers as grew nowhere else. Witch flowers, Sula had named them, in her own language, and would not touch them nor go near the well. She only had to walk within yards of it and she began to shiver. Her brown eyes, so like those of the seals, held fright in their depths yet she could not explain her fear.

She never saw Gwyn watching her. He was too cunning. But she knew he watched, for she knew there were human eyes in the bushes. She did not mind the eyes of bird or beast. She would never stay alone; Hugh had always to be within call and when he drove the donkey and cart to the village for supplies, she went with him, dressed always in the deep blues and greens of the sea, her long black hair sleek against her head and sliding softly down her back.

The old women saw her and made the sign of the cross, warding off the evil eye. Some of them spat into the wind to avert the devil in her, and Sula, who had known the fear of witches in her own land, was saddened, for there was no harm in her, but she could not reach out and tell them. Nor would they come near.

She knew the language of flowers; and she knew the worth of herbs and simples: prodwort for happiness; mushrooms for suspicion; nettles for cruelty; rowan for prudence; dragonwort for hatred. She picked the flowers and made posies and gave them to Hugh — but he could not read the messages and did not understand. Later came other flowers: limes for love; jasmine for grace and honeysuckle for bonds more binding than marriage vows. She could brew a healing lotion for a stye on the eye, or a septic cut on a finger. She could brew a tea that would soothe to sleep, or bring relief to aching muscles, and the herbs she put in her bath kept her skin soft and supple. She was darker than the women in the village, her skin the soft creamy toffee tan of a Jersey cow, and even the women began to say it was the colour of a seal hide when the fur was removed.

And Gwyn, smiling crookedly, added to the tales, telling how she changed into a seal in the sea at night and swam with the pups. He enjoyed this new power. The villagers listened avidly. And how she did not need a fur to wrap her, but the fur grew as the waves thrust against her, and vanished when she came on land for truly she was an evil woman with many powers.

No knowledge of the talk reached Hugh though he knew the village was less friendly now. His world was small and safe and serene and he did not need others. He showed Sula where the deer came to feed. She called them softly and they trusted her, for she was almost as much a wild thing as they and the fawns came to her hands and took food from her.

This too Gwyn saw.

She was a fairy thing, a changeling from a wickeder world.

He helped his curse to come true by the whispered spite of his tongue and by clever words. Men who did not trust him, believed him, because there was so little to believe in the village where day after day was the same, with no great events to lighten the dullness of living. There was nothing to talk about but themselves, and the new litter of piglets at Morgan Jones' farm, and the cow calf born to Evans the Post, and the baby due to Megan Pritchard, and how Megan wanted a little daughter but Maldwyn had set his heart on a little boy.

So there was excitement in talking about the seal woman and the strangeness of her coming, for Gwyn had told them that there on the beach that first day was no woman at all but two seals, dark and shining, oil covered, under the first night stars. Then, when Hugh had lifted them and taken them to his hut, and bathed the big seal in strange unguents which he had put in the bath water, there had come from it, not a seal but this girl creature, speaking strange words like a seal calling to its young. Each morning, Gwyn said, she went to the seal pen and put down her nose to the pups, and they raised their heads to greet her and kiss her, as they kissed their mothers.

The children thought it was exciting, that a woman could go down to the sea and swim and become a seal again. Maybe one day she and the pups would go and leave Hugh desolate for surely no man should take a seal thing to wife. They had gone to the shore and watched her swim but saw nothing unusual.

The stories spread and grew.

And then were almost forgotten.

Disaster came to the village.

Gryfydd Evans had a brother a long way away, over the border in England. Wyn Evans also bred pigs. His pigs were the best in Cheshire, and were sold for high prices in the markets and men sought for breeding stock from him. Wyn wrote to Gryff and that was a rare event, for Gryff never got a letter except from the income tax people and the electricity people and the gas people and the rates; only annoying letters from people wanting money. Never exciting letters telling him news for his sons were busy in Canada with no time to write, and his daughter in Australia had almost forgotten home except at Christmas.

So when Evans the Post brought the letter it was a great event, and Gryff gave him a cup of tea and bara brydd from the last baking, made by Angharad who came up every day to clean the house and cook for him. He opened the letter and told Evans about the wonderful brood sow his brother was offering him. In return he wanted a young boar that was the best son Titanic had ever fathered. Wyn had too many sows and Gryff did not need another boar yet, for Titanic was far from old and the best boar he had ever bought, so that his sows had fourteen and sixteen little pigs at a time, and each piglet thrived.

Gryff took his battered old Land Rover and drove to Cheshire that very day and brought back the sow, leaving the young boar in exchange.

She was a fine big sow and she was due to farrow soon and there would be more piglets on the farm.

But neither Wyn nor Gryff knew of the sorrow that was in store; for the sow had picked up an infection, and she sickened and died, almost at once. And Dafydd Parry the vet came and did not know how to say that the sow had brought swine fever to the village and all Gryff's beautiful pigs must be killed.

No man in the village might sell a pig, or move a pig from one place to another.

Nothing so terrible had ever happened in the village.

Truly someone had put a curse on them all.

Truly, Gwyn said, and hid his triumph when he heard the sad tale in the inn at night. For had not the evil started with the seal woman, and was not she the cause of their trouble? The wickedness of bringing her to the mountain must be expiated. She must be driven back to the sea from which she came. And her evil brood with her. It was not natural for seals to live with men, living like dogs on the hearth rug.

The village listened. They did not like Gwyn and they were not cruel people. They could not judge the woman yet; she had not been near them. But curses did not need the presence of those who cursed, Gwyn said, his face sly, as he thought of the slate at the bottom of the cursing well, and the wickedness he had already brought on Gryff in return for his tongue lashing.

The swine fever spread.

Soon there was not a living pig left in the village and the air was angry with the smell of burned carcases for only fire could remove the evil. Pig styes were burned down and new ones built, for one day there would be more pigs in the village; one day they would be free from infection. They could not pass it on, for they were too isolated.

Within months the place would be declared free again. New pigs would come, but meanwhile no one had livestock to tend, except for the few cows kept for milking. The sheep on the mountains too, which lived almost wild, only checked at rare intervals when the lambs were born, or when the sheep were dipped, or the lambs were marked, or the ewes were with the rams, or the wool was sheared.

There was nothing to do but meet on the street

corners by day and in the inn by night, and to talk.

The talk grew wild. Gwyn thought of the talk as a tiny fire, just starting in a thicket. It needed fanning, and more wood added, until, one day, it would grow to a roaring forest fire, out of control, destroying everything it touched. He thought of fire; of red flames on the mountain and the wind fanning them until Hugh's home was burned to a cinder and the valley around the cursing well was blasted and flowerless, burnt and sere. Fire excited him.

He did not know of the wishing well, for that was only known to a very few; and even some of those did not believe it for they had never found the entrance. Only those who were small and slight could reach the well. Children always found the entrance; but as they grew older, some discovered that the way they had once known was blocked and they could not get through. Then they forgot, believing it had been a wonderful dream. Those that were denied the hidden valley and the sunshine and the flowers were sad for something they had lost, but they did not know what until their children in their turn found the hidden entrance and came back to tell them of the marvels they had seen — the creaming water and the sparkling torrent that bubbled over weathered rocks. There was singing in the valley, and bird noise. The deer there did not run when they saw people for they sensed these people were gentle and understood animals and would not hurt them.

Children played happily together by the wishing well, and some wished for a dog; and sometimes a puppy came to the child's home; and some wished for a cat and found a new kitten; and some wished for worldly goods and money to buy goods and for other riches, and for them the tunnel was gone for ever. They could never find its mouth again, nor come to play with the other children.

6

Winter came.

Sula, who had found the long hot days too tiring, began to sing around the place. With the first hard frost came boundless energy and an excitement that Hugh did not understand, for as yet she had few words of his language and he could not master hers. She could not tell him that the rime on the grass reminded her of her home; of the snow covered hills and the barren valleys and the green water, deep under the ice that sparkled and glittered as the sun sparkled now on grass that was white and beautiful, turning the valley to another place, another world.

The frost went and the next day dawned warm and sunny.

Sun glittered in the sea. White waves creamed soothingly on the shore and Tomas and Tonto were restless, wanting to swim. Sula had made herself a reed pipe and played to the seals. She played soft tunes in the evenings to Hugh, who listened, his face rapt, for like all his countrymen he loved music.

It was easier to talk in song than with words, for he could teach her the tunes he loved, by singing them softly to her. Sometimes the villagers, passing on the cliffs, heard the sweet wild music and Hugh's deep voice, and shuddered, thinking of wickedness there in the glen and of faery spells, that would bring yet more sorrow. Gwyn had told them of wizardry, and how Sula had cursed the village and brought misfortune.

For the death of the pigs had brought too much sorrow, for pigs were their wealth. Without them little money came to the village. The women had no money to buy wool to make clothes. They went into the fields and collected the sheep wool from the hedges and spun it and dyed it and wove it as they had in the old days.

They had too much time on their hands.

They talked.

Little words without much meaning.

Words that changed as they went from one mouth to another.

Words that started as small lies and became big ones.

As small evils that became big ones.

Where there was talk, there was always Gwyn, watching, waiting, his crooked smile ready to add what words might not add; reminding people that with the coming of the seal woman the oil had come to the beaches and the summer visitors had kept away, because the beaches were not clean. And summer tourists brought money to the village.

Gwyn went into the big town and there in a shop window saw the cloths that Sula had embroidered, priced high. They were beautiful, more beautiful than any work that the village women could do, for Sula's mother had been famous for her embroidery and had taught her daughter well. Sula made her own clothes; and they too branded her as outlandish for she made the clothes she had always worn. Fine embroidered blouses worn under dark blue dresses that brushed the ground, the bodice laced with gay ribbons. Matching ribbons tied back her long black hair. She was strange and exotic and beautiful, and the women did not trust her. The men did not speak of her, but their eyes watched her as she passed. She was like no woman they had ever seen.

On this fine day after the frost, Sula went to the beach with the seals, and both Tonto and Tomas took to the sea. Soon they must return to the sea. She began to play, a soft tune from long ago, a tune her mother had played as Sula lay in her wooden cradle, rocked by her mother's foot, and her mother sang of lost love, of men lost at sea, of dark nights, of loneliness. Sula was homesick for her parents and her little brothers. They had been good days, when she was young, with laughter and dancing sometimes, and long winter nights filled with rejoicing at a wedding or a birthday, or sorrow at a death. They had stayed in the ice lands for a long time. She wished they had stayed for ever.

They were good people. Simple people. People who cared about one another and helped one another when times were hard and shared their bounty when the fishing was good. When a child was born all blessed the child and brought it salt and silver, and one of the beautiful fan shells that were found on the summer beaches in the brief short halcyon days; and a seabird's egg, for fortune.

She would have been married by now in her own land. She thought sometimes of her man; they had been betrothed for two years. He too had died when the savage guns spoke their bitter message. Now she was wed in a strange land and she did not even know where her own land lay far over the sea. She looked out to sea as if the waves could tell her of her home. She did not want to return — and yet — it was lonely here except for Hugh. She had no women to talk to: she longed for talk of flowers and recipes, of sewing and knitting, and of children growing as the flowers grew.

She saw the dark heads at sea. Tomas and Tonto; and more besides. Her seals were playing, far out

46

beyond the breakers, but when she raised the pipe to her lips they turned and headed towards her. Behind them came four more seals; their dark heads' cresting the water, lifted in wonder listening to the soft singing. They had never heard music before.

Tomas and Tonto loved the music and, coming from the water waddled over the beach and lay at her feet, one head on each thigh, brown eyes watching her face, as she played the soft long-ago songs her mother had sung, and the four seal cows came closer, and closer, until they lay at the edge of the waves, rapt, their bodies swaying in time to the tune.

Hugh watched her, smiling. He too had once played to the seals on another beach not so far from here. He did not know that these seals came from the beach for more oil had drifted there and their feeding places were fouled. The cows had left dead pups behind, choked by the oil that covered nose and eyes and poured into their mouths.

Sula was aware of watching hostile eyes. She did not know where. She put away the pipe. The seals, startled by her movement, slipped back into the sea. She watched the four dark heads swim away and then turned and spoke lazily to Tonto and Tomas who had proved as intelligent as dogs and understood her when she said 'come' or called out to them, in her own tongue, 'Tonto, Tomas, food.'

Gwyn was hidden behind a thorn bush. Now he had a tale to tell for the woman had brought more of her own kind out of the sea with her magic, playing tunes of a strangeness such as no man ever heard. Tonight in the vaults, he would tell the old men what he had seen.

They would go home and tell their wives who would tell their sons and daughters.

The word would spread.

But he needed more; more fuel for the flames he was fanning.

Next day he found what he needed, for one of the village children, playing too close to the cliff edge, slipped and fell and broke a leg. Sula was near and would have run to help, but the other children screamed, and their mothers came running and one of them turned on her and rated her for a witch, casting the evil eye, and spat at her.

It was an age old sign; a world-wide sign and Sula knew it. She turned away, and the seals followed her, knowing she was hurt, wanting to console her. Tonto butted her with his head and Tomas swayed behind her, trying to get close.

Her walk was almost a run.

Hugh had seen the women. He was watching them, his face dismayed, for he had not realized that their hatred was growing. But they could do no harm, he consoled himself, and words did not kill.

It would blow over. He had been part of the valley for so long now, he did not want to move away. He put an arm round Sula, and they walked to the hut, the seals behind them. The four of them entered the door and shut it tight against ill will, hatred and superstition.

A stone rattled against the door.

Sula closed the curtains and built up the fire.

She was very cold.

Fear had come to her, and it had come to stay for she did not know what she had done to anger the people. If only she could talk to the women; they would surely not fear her then, alone here in a strange land, where nobody spoke as she spoke and where her customs were not their customs.

That night she began to embroider a new cloth.

Hugh watched her, wondering, not knowing that on

48

it she was making the story of the gentle people of her holiday land, and their belief in God who helped all, and her embroidery was a prayer for help.

'You are sad?' Hugh asked. She had learned a little of his tongue now.

She smiled at him. He should not know how she felt. He had been good to her and she loved him now, and would never leave him.

In the inn that night Gwyn was speaking.

'Did you see?' he asked. 'The seals that came to the shore to talk with her. And do you see how Hugh grows ever younger; he was an old man. Yet now his step is spry and he laughs and talks like a young man. Is that not a sign of evil?'

The old men nodded, but Gryff the farmer who had come down to the inn for a drink, away from his quiet place where no pigs squealed, listened in horror.

'She means no harm,' he said. 'She has a way with beasts. And her coming has eased Hugh's sorrow.'

Gwyn laughed.

It was not a pleasant sound, and even the old men who had been nodding their heads as they smoked their pipes, were momentarily uneasy.

'She brought the oil to the beaches; and the fever to the pigs; and now she casts her wicked eye on the children who play on the cliffs,' Gwyn said.

'Children fell on the cliffs before she came,' Gryff said. He was a small man, grey-haired, grey-moustached, with quiet blue eyes that looked deep into a man. He preached of hellfire, but he also preached of charity.

'Your talk is devil talk and evil,' he said.

Gwyn hated him even more, remembering how Gryff had scolded him before; had talked of the hell-fires waiting and the evil that would catch up with him.

49

'Do not listen,' Gryff said to the old men. They did not meet his eyes. They knew that when Sunday came he would preach passionately of the evils of gossip and of lying tongues, and of the wickedness of envy and of malice.

And they knew that when Monday came they would forget his words and sit with their heads close together and let the talk grow. Talk never did harm.

Sticks and stones could break all bones, but words could never hurt folk.

Words.

Only Gwyn knew their real use; to twist meaning, to put a thought of malice or envy where none had been before, to suggest, to connive.

Gwyn's own mind was so twisted that he could see no good in anyone. Should a man make him a gift, he would think the man bribing him, to do something for that man; should a man give him kindness, he would look behind it for a meanness; should a man offer him bread and comfort he would wonder what the man had done wrong, that he must make up to Gwyn, whom men scorned.

But men would not always scorn him.

He would rid the village of the evil that had come to it and restore its prosperity.

He would rid them of the seal woman.

Then he would retrieve the curse slate from the deep water of the well; and when the sun shone fair and the pigs grew fat and the people thrived they would thank him and admit he was a greater man than they. They would honour him; him, twisted Gwyn with the legs that would never carry him straight, and the black magic in him his mother had taught him. He would be a great man. And all because he knew the power of words.

'No mortal woman ever looked like that,' he said.

Gwyn had gone.

The old men nodded, for Sula was beautiful and alien; darker than the women of the village; darkness due to the seal fur that was hers each night when she went down to the beach and swam with her own kind.

Gwyn has seen her in her seal shape, he said, with sly looks. And he had looked through the window and seen Hugh sleeping in his chair, in a sleep that was enchantment, from the herbs she picked by day, and that was never natural.

Hugh was to be pitied and to be rescued from her.

How, Gwyn did not say.

The old men went home.

Sometimes, in the night, when they could not sleep, they felt an unease, a stirring of anxiety, for the talk was growing ever wilder; and there were plans now, plans that Gwyn put into their heads and into their mouths.

These things were wrong.

Then came the vivid pictures of Sula swimming with the seals and they knew they were not wrong. Just as they knew that Ianto in the valley, a little dried up stick of a man who lived alone and fired his shotgun at anyone who came near, was in reality the wolf dog that plagued the farmers on the hills and ripped out throats from the lambs, and fed on blood.

They had found the evidence on Ianto's land; the dead lambs; dragged and worried and torn.

And there was Megan-Gwyn's fourth cousin, at the smallholding, with her herbs and simples too. It did not do to cross Megan for if you did the children ailed and the cows sickened. So Megan lived well on food given her and clothes given her, and went on making love potions for the girls that came to her, wanting to catch themselves a lad for life, and not for just a little courting at a dance or a wedding.

Gwyn no longer spoke of his horse, he wanted men

51

to believe him, and though he knew the horse came nightly, it was invisible to all but him.

He needed to plan. He watched Sula constantly and she grew more afraid.

Fear was with her constantly for she knew without words that he was evil.

7

They had never known such wild weather.

Storm bred storm; rain spilled out of clouds that almost brushed the fields; the mountains were hidden. The wind screamed down the valley; it tore tiles from the roofs and destroyed a barn; it blew haystacks onto the shore; it piled the sea into a great tide that spilled over the land.

The river spread its banks and flooded the fields. The haystacks were soaked and hay went mouldy; the winter wheat was spoiled and lay flat on the sodden ground.

The wind never eased.

Daylong, nightlong, it screamed round the houses, flailed the trees, hurled itself against the mountains. The peaks were gone; there was only cloud. High banks of black cloud, from which the rain poured unceasingly, as if it would never stop.

God had sent the rain to flood the world for its wickedness, and there was no Noah.

The sea was over the sands; the sea was over the lower cliffs; the sea was invading the summer houses, beating against their doors, creeping under their doors, leaving, when the tide went out, a sodden smelling mass of soaked carpet, of tiles dislodged from their base; of weed piled high against the doors.

The summer people were lucky, for they did not

know. They would live the winter in innocence and only next year would they find out what happened.

The village people knew.

Never had the sea come so high.

Never had the wind been so strong.

Never had the river spilled over its banks before.

Children went to school by boat; men in boats ferried along the river street, bringing provisions, taking those who were in danger from the water to the church hall, and there the people congregated with nothing to do but talk.

Talk of the evil spreading through the village.

Talk of the seal woman, the witch woman, the woman from the sea. She lived by the cursing well; perhaps her own curse craft bobbed daily on the water as she wished evil on those around her. They had never harmed her. Why should she harm them?

They thought of her now with growing hatred; of her strange soft singing, the seal songs of her seal people, of her long dark hair and her brown seal eyes. But the villagers did not see those eyes were so full of sorrow at times.

They knew their thoughts were nonsense; yet what was nonsense and what was the truth?

There were men who at a thought could bend a steel fork in two; there were those who could conjure up the dead; there was Ynys in the village who could tell the future and tell each girl which lad she would wed; could foresee disaster. Ynys had spoken of an evil among the pigs. Sometimes they laughed at her, but now they remembered uneasily how she had spoken of bad times coming, long ago, when life was good. She spoke of a stranger coming to live among them — a stranger who would bring ill luck to the people.

Before the seal woman was washed ashore.

Rain lashed down steadily, blurring the outside

world, isolating them even more. No one could reach the valley. No one could leave the valley. Not even by sea, for the waves were too wild for any boat to be launched.

The village shop ran out of flour and there was no bread.

Living grew hard; and still it rained.

A group of helicopters flew over and dropped sacks of food, and life was eased, but still it rained.

The water lay sullen and grey, slow moving, sluggish, on the fields and out of the water poked banks of sere grass; bushes, sodden with wet; and trees that had no right to be in water. Cattle were marooned. Sheep were drowned. The fields were white with gulls that had come inland, away from the terrifying suck and snarl of water on the beaches.

Water.

In the summer they had drought, and now there was water everywhere. No one could visit Gryff Evans, who was above the floods, but safe in his warm stone farmhouse. His deep freeze was full and he had flour in plenty and he was snug, but he was worried, for he knew that the weather would add fuel to the fires that Gwyn was stoking, and he knew Gwyn for a terrible envious man who would stop at nothing to win his way. He feared that Gwyn had a madness inside him. But Gwyn was clever and cunning and had found a way to be heard.

And there were those who were easy to lead.

Some of the lads were as wild as Gwyn and could plot mischief. Gryff could smell mischief; fire and brimstone, a rumour from hell.

He preached against it every Sunday, but now he could not reach the chapel. Geraint Jones who would preach in his stead was an innocent man, seeing no evil, unaware of the depths within men, aware only of the smiling surface that hid unknown sins from the light.

He was a good man, a simple man, and he was never included in the gossip, for he did not believe such things could be. He did not believe that Gwyn would steal, even when Gwyn was put in jail. Geraint knew there had been a mistake. He did not believe that the children in his class would lie, even when he found them out.

The children mocked him, playing up in his lessons, laughing at his stammer and his bright colour when they plagued him more than usual. He longed for school to end each week, and he came hopefully each Monday sure that this week would be better.

It never was.

His preachings would not raise one tiny prick of conscience, Gryff knew.

They needed his thunder at their wickedness.

He stood at the window of his farmhouse, looking down on the floods. Only the hedges showed where the fields had been. His cattle were safe in his barn. He went out to milk, but even as he milked, he worried, wanting no harm to come to Hugh and the girl from across the sea. He had seen her sadness, and had thought how strange it must be for her to come to this land, far from her own land, and live among strangers, unable to speak to them or to understand their ways.

He had seen her plait garlands of wild flowers to deck the house that was now more than a hut, for Hugh had built on to it. They had four rooms and a good strong roof; and a fireplace where they burned driftwood cast up on the beach. Hugh had used stone, taken from the ruins of old cottages on the moors.

They needed to buy very little for Hugh grew fruit and vegetables; and the goat he kept gave them milk and cheese; and the hens he kept gave them eggs. Sula picked the blackberries from the hedges for jam and jelly and pies. She picked the sloes and made a sweet drink from them, and she found a colony of bees and housed them in a straw skip that she made with her own hands, and now they had honey.

There were hazel nuts on the bushes.

There was bilberry, and in summer she had planted little wild strawberries that were sweeter than any bought in a shop.

Hugh caught fish for all of them; for Tonto and Tomas and for himself and Sula. They did not eat meat and this too gave cause for comment for did not the seal woman eat like a seal, living on fish? She ate it raw, they said, eyeing one another to see if the story was believed; she ate it live, some said, embroidering on the lie, for effect, to make it dramatic, to make it a better story than others had told.

The stories grew; they spread, each one adding a little word here, a small twist there, until they were unrecognizable, and some of those that heard them wished the tales had never started.

Others enjoyed them.

It was exciting to think of a woman living among them as this woman did, so alien, so strange, so different.

She could not be mortal for she did everything too well. Her sewing was wonderful to see; the little scenes alive under her needle, the clothes and aprons embroidered with running deer, bobbing rabbits, strange shaped houses and children oddly dressed.

Hugh took them in the summer to the shop in the big town on the other side of the pass, and here the tourists loved them; and he brought back material with him for more sewing; and wool to knit into thick warm jerseys. Sula, pleased to be able to help him finance their home, made gloves and socks and round caps and scarves, in a stitch her mother had taught her that was like no stitch seen in the village.

With the wind and the rain and the scouring tides came more seal pups, flung up on the beaches. Sula and Hugh soon had five seals round the house. One of these had been badly cut by broken glass, and cried like a baby for Sula to comfort her, crawling towards her, rubbing against her legs.

Gwyn, from his hidden eyrie, saw this and told of it in the inn that night.

What further proof did they need?

She would bring more evil.

But what could they do?

They did not know.

Gwyn had ideas, but he wanted to wait. When the floods went, when the rain eased, where the fields dried, there would be much to see; the dead beasts to count; the cost to reckon. The aftermath to deal with.

Hugh and Sula had never been so busy.

They were isolated by the floods, except for Gwyn, who used a small boat to reach his spying place.

The five seals were always so hungry and it was not easy to catch fish in the stormy weather. Hugh hung nets over the rocks, and brought them in daily; there were fish there, but never enough.

They ate eggs and they ate cheese and gave the fish to the seals.

When the evenings were long Sula played to them; she sang softly, and the seals came to listen. Hugh had added a very big room to the side of the hut; there was little furniture in it. Two chairs and a table, and a rug by the fire, and the rest of the floor was free for the seals to play.

Sula taught them to catch balls; to flip balls to one another. Tomas swayed to the music, Tonto danced in circles, and clapped his flippers; the new seals from the sea watched with interest and the little female crooned softly in time to the music. Hugh had never laughed so much.

He spent his time making more furniture; carving tiny seals and horses that he took with Sula's embroidery to the shop on the far side of the pass. He discovered he could make the animals look as if they were alive, and rows of little deer marched across the mantelpiece above the fireplace.

Sula drew the animals for him and he copied them.

Late one night, when the fire had almost died and the seals had been put in their sleeping place beyond the house, there came a whine at the door.

Sula opend it.

A small collie bitch stood there, a newborn puppy in her mouth.

Sula called her in, and found a box and put her in it, and in the next three hours four more pups were born. Sula fed her. She was starvation thin, her sides gaunt, each rib showing. Her paws were red and raw.

Sula bathed them with a lotion made from elder leaves steeped overnight. She bound them with damp leaves, to soothe them. So had her people done in their home. The doctors knew better than college lore; they used the old ways, and the old ways often worked. And if they did not work, it was the will of God, and no man could gainsay Him.

The bitch was soaked. She had been swimming.

That night Gwyn went home and called to his collie bitch but there was no answer. He went into the shed where she was kept. The rope that held her was gnawed right through and a tunnel under the tumbledown side of the wooden hut showed where she had escaped. The dried up stale food on her plate was untouched. He was angrier than he had ever been for she was in whelp and each pup alone was worth twenty pounds, to the right man. People wanted good collies. Five pups at twenty pounds each was a hundred pounds and more money than Gwyn had ever owned at one time.

He would find her, and find her pups.

He did find her, three days later, when he saw her lying outside Hugh's home in the sunshine. The rain had stopped at last and the waters were falling. The fields were drying. The bitch lay quiet, happy for the first time in her life, with no one to shout at her, or kick her or throw his boots at her. She loved her pups and nursed them devotedly, and when Sula came with food she shook the babies from her and leaped up at the woman who had rescued her and who fed her good food and was kind to her, wagging her tail as if it would come off.

She had never greeted Gwyn like that.

The hatred he had been feeding grew even more monstrous.

The woman should suffer.

He would get those pups back, but not until they were old enough to sell. Let her feed them up; she would feed them well. He could see that the bitch was already plumper.

So the woman would make an enemy of him deliberately; would steal his collie; that was a tale to tell overnight when the inn opened. Up to now he had only guesses to throw into the conversation. Now he had facts. She had spirited the bitch away deliberately, had enticed her, had swum through the flood and dug into the hut to get her for the ground was too hard for the bitch to dig her way out. He did not know that the collie had always upset her water bowl, filled with musty water, in the same place, and so softened the ground.

That night in the inn Gwyn was eloquent, telling them how his collie had been charmed away from him.

Even the old men, knowing **Gwyn**, wondered a little; it was hard to believe any dog could attach itself to this man as he said the dog had been attached, adoring him, obeying him, following him everywhere.

There was one way Gwyn could show his hatred. He could show Hugh.

That night he took a cork from the inn, and he wrote a curse upon a piece of paper; he wrote it carefully and he wrote it well, and he cursed Sula the seal woman from today to eternity, wishing her every ill he could imagine, wishing her death by flames.

Next morning Hugh found the curse craft.

He took it out of the water and read it, and felt sick.

That anyone could so hate his wife; his gentle wife, who knew nothing of wickedness; who loved animals and quiet places, and sitting at his side, trying to learn his language.

He sprinkled holy water on the craft and added the sign of the cross and released it on the water. Its work would never be done now, but for all that there was someone who hated her so much that he could place his curse where he knew Hugh would see it.

Hugh thought of the faces of the villagers, turned away from him; of the shopkeepers, dealing with him swiftly, as if they wanted him out of their shops, fast. Of the women, watching with closed faces and stony eyes as Sula passed them, in her bright blouses, embroidered at throat and cuff, and the gay laced dress. Her hair was always tied back with a ribbon that matched her dress; he loved to buy her ribbons and see her tie them into big bows, taking such care to get each side even, yet she was not vain. They had no mirror in the house, nor did she ever bend to look at herself in the waters of the wells.

She was playing now with the puppies. They ran after her and teased at her dress hem and she pushed the little things away, laughing, telling them no, for that would tear her clothes.

Tonto loved the puppies; Tomàs was wary of them, and the other seals were kept away. They were, as yet, wild things, and might harm them. And the collie mother did not like the seals too near her young, though she bore with Tonto who thought she was a new playmate for him and tried to tease her into play.

One morning when the pups were almost five weeks old, the collie did begin to play. She chased Tonto and then he turned and chased her. Gwyn, hidden in his bush, saw them, and knew that here was more wickedness. It was not natural for a dog to play with a seal.

He did not need the boat to get to the inn that night. By next day everyone was talking about the collie that played with the seals; all the seals, and ate fish with them; and how the pups and the seal slept together in a pile, and the woman curled herself round all of them, and sang her spells.

She was a witch as well as a seal woman.

Prove it, one man said.

Gwyn would prove it.

That night he stole Mina, a black cat from one of the village houses, as she sat watching the moon, waiting for mice to emerge from the crevices of the alley wall. He put her in a sack, and he took the sack, tied by the throat and put it on Hugh's doorstep.

Sula heard the cat crying and took her in and fed her. She fed her fish, and cream from the goat milk, and put her in a warm basket by the fire. Mina's home had not been a good one; she was put out at night; was never allowed by the fire and was fed on scraps. She had never been so well fed.

She decided to stay.

Black cats and witches went together, Gwyn said.

Even if the witch were a seal woman.

There were no witches, some said. Others knew better; for even today, the newspapers told of witches meeting in covens on Midsummer night, by the standing stones; of witches in the woods at Alderley Edge where the Wizard Rock bore testimony to its age old use; of white witches who healed; and of black witches who sold curses and potions.

The old ways lived on. The Black Mass was still celebrated in some places, and the old evils persisted.

Gwyn found the old cuttings he had kept, telling of witchcraft in England; in Scotland; even in Wales. He had cuttings about poltergeists and about men and women possessed of the devil; about priests brought in to exorcise wickedness.

If such thing happened, so could the seal woman be a witch. There were witches. The newspapers said so and did not they always tell the truth?

One man listened as Gryff had listened. He was a newspaper reporter and he was aware of more wickedness than even Gwyn knew. Words crossed his mind unbidden, as Gwyn talked on, words from a poem by Chesterton, written about Fleet Street; which the poet thought of as Hell.

'And all the truth they talk in Hell
And all the lies they write.'

Here, he knew, a man was talking lies. But how to stop him?

'She was washed overboard from some boat, poor woman. You should feel pity for her, alone in a strange land, far from her own people,' he said.

He was a stranger and had no right to speak.

Cold eyes looked through him. He might not have been there. The chill of their dislike made him shiver and he drank his beer quickly and went out into the night. He was staying with Gryff Evans, whose father

63

had known the reporter's grandfather, long ago when both were young. Bill Harrison's grandfather had often told him of the farm in the mountains; and told him to go there when life was cruel and he needed peace.

He had come for peace, looking down on the quiet village with its small houses and pretty gardens. Here he would find kindness, he thought; gentleness, with time to spare for strangers; with no pressures as there were in the big cities.

He had sat at night, for almost a week, in the inn and what he had heard appalled him. For here was no tenderness, no sympathy, no understanding. Only malice, fostered by a clever wicked man; and the stories spreading, like poison in a pool. A festering mass of hatred and envy; of antagonism against the unknown woman who had been so unfortunate.

Yet nobody thought of her.

They vied with their wild tales that grew wilder as the beer soaked in; stories inspired by fear of the unknown; stories inspired by the high flying tongues made stupid with too much to drink; made fuddled and unwise as their brains and their wits addled; telling wilder and wilder stories, inventing even more stupendous lies, until it was no longer a gentle woman who lived by the cursing well, but evil incarnate, hot from Hell, come to destroy them all.

He had thought that charity and kindness lived in lonely places.

But the people were as bad as those in cities; cruel tongued and bitter with dislike, ready to believe ill of all men and far more ill of those who were strangers. As he was a stranger. He had turned back as he left the inn; the men were silent, watching him. He was aware of their hostile eyes as he walked up the mountain. He did not breathe deeply till he reached Gryff, and Gryff

64

smiled at him. They sat in friendly silence, not needing words and watched the tabby cat clean her kitten.

Next morning, he left the village. His stay was ended. It was time to return to work.

8

The village was busy cleaning up after the floods. No time for talk.

Sula watched the puppies grow.

The bitch followed Sula everywhere she went, once the pups were old enough to leave. Gwyn, spying, was seized with even worse envy for the bitch had never followed him, or shown him the least affection. Everywhere that Sula went, also went Tonto and Tomas and the bitch that she had named Topsy.

The collie played with the seals, and the pups played with all the animals, learning not to bite too hard, or Tonto and Tomas roared at them, and Topsy slapped them.

There was even more laughter in the little house.

Gwyn tried to plan but could think of no plan.

He had no work to do; sometimes at night he netted a hare, spreading his snare by the five-barred gate, knowing the hare paths. Sometimes he snared a rabbit, careful not to be caught for the snares were illegal.

Perhaps he could snare a seal.

Or snare a pup.

But one night in the inn, talking of his collie bitch and the way she had been enticed by witchcraft, Aelwyn the Bread asked him why he had not reported the seal woman to the police for theft. She had stolen the bitch, surely, and the pups were valuable.

Dai the Police was astounded when Gwyn walked into the little office at the back of his house. Dai's parish was a big one. He had twenty villages to care for, and could be many miles away when needed. But he was rarely needed. Gwyn was more likely to run from the police than seek them out. He listened as Gwyn told him how the woman living with Hugh had stolen his bitch.

Dai knew the bitch and a sorry looking creature she was, with, he was certain, the marks of heavy boots on her ribs, and as well fed as a starving kitten. More likely she had taken off and found fatter feeding elsewhere. But the pups were worth money, here in farming country, where every man needed a sheep dog and most men kept a few sheep.

Dai kept nine ewes himself, in the tiny paddock at the back of the house.

He had no sheep dog, having no time to train it, so he gave his ewes names, and every morning visited them with titbits, handfeeding them, so they would come when he called, and he could watch them for foot rot and other ills. The village laughed at him, seeing him in the field with the ewes running to him, coming to their names; Megan and Bronwen, and their daughters, wanting to be stroked and petted, eating the crusts that Dai's wife cut off the bread. Their wool and their lambs helped pay for the children's clothes, for Dai's three sons were all at the age when they grew as you looked at them, showing ankle and wrist almost before the newness had worn off their school blazers.

He had a pet dog; a little Jack Russell/Collie cross, petted and made much of. He had always felt sorry for Gwyn's collie, and now he wished that Gwyn had not come to him, for it was certain the little beast had a better home.

But Dai would have to find out.

He had never been to the cursing well. Long ago he too had visited the wishing well, and wondered if it was still possible to crawl to it along the narrow tunnel. He remembered it with a sigh; it had been a sunny day and there had been deer in the valley and little bright finches, and bluetits flying. He had wished for what? He could not remember, but most of his wishes had come true, for he was a happy man, with a wife and three sons and nine fat ewes, all now in lamb again. And mostly, he liked his work, for there was little real crime in the villages and he knew his people well.

They knew Dai and never gossiped in his hearing, for he was a hard man on those who spoke evil of others.

Hugh greeted him with a smile that changed to a worried frown when Dai told how Gwyn had accused Sula of stealing the bitch.

'She came to us on the first night of the floods, and we thought she was a stray,' he said.

Sula, coming round the corner of the house, the seals at her heels, and the bitch, and the five pups, stopped and smiled at Dai. He had heard the stories about her; the seal woman from the sea. He knew they were nonsense. She had a grace about her that was not shared by the women in the valley. She was gentle and she was kind. She still spoke little of any tongue but her own, but as she passed him she said shyly, 'I make tea,' and vanished into the house.

Dai, following Hugh indoors, was fascinated for he had never seen a home like this. The big room with the two chairs and the table, and the big bare floor where the animals played, had been transformed. Hugh had painted the walls white, and on them Sula had drawn pictures of her dream country. A country of snow and ice; of seals in green waters; of small steep-roofed houses, and of towering snow-covered mountains.

The scenes were so real he could visualize her

country, far across the sea. People on the walls smiled at him, with kind faces; he did not know that they were Sula's mother and her father and her little brother, dressed from head to foot in furs, a small round bundle with a happy laughing face and bright black eyes that seemed to watch Dai as he turned away. She had nothing to remind her of them except her memory.

A wood fire burned on the hearth and on the mantelpiece were Hugh's wooden carvings; seal and bear and tiger, horse and dog and cat, carefully worked in wood, the grain polished till the light caught it and the animals seemed to dance along. There was an easy flow about them, as if their legs would move, their heads would turn, their eyes would light with life.

'She was starving, and she was hurt when she came to us,' Hugh said. 'It would be sad if she went back to her master. He did not value her. I will buy her; and give him the money when I sell the pups. If he does not agree, I think that the RSPCA inspector might be interested in what I have to say.'

'I'll ask him,' Dai said.

He had a thought or two of his own for he had known the bitch when Gwyn owned her, and he had not recognized her. She was well fed, her coat gleaming, her eyes bright, in spite of her recent whelping; she followed Sula with her eyes even when she did not follow her with her legs, and she obeyed every gesture.

'Can you find good buyers for the pups?' Hugh asked.

'One for my boys,' Dai said. 'And one for Gryff Evans, who was saying that his collie is old and he is looking for a pup to bring on. Gwyn found the bitch a nuisance; if you can offer him enough money . . .'

'I will sew, and you will carve,' Sula said, looking up as she poured the tea. She handed Dai little cakes; such cakes as he had never tasted before, made of honey and crushed nuts and iced with patterns of tiny flowers. She loved to embroider everything she did; even the food, and Hugh sometimes laughed at her and teased her for it. The chairs were backed with rich cloths, the windows hung with embroidered curtains; a patterned cloth covered the tables. Seals played all over it; seals swimming and diving through green water, seaweed fronds so real that Dai expected them to wave in the wind. Brown seal eyes watched him from the corner of the room and the collie pups watched the stranger, a little wary for they did not see many people. Few came to the valley.

'I remember the wishing well,' Dai said wistfully. 'My younger son still visits it. I doubt if I could crawl through the tunnel now.' He patted his paunch. 'I sit too much, writing reports about nothing.' He laughed.

'They say the well only works for those who believe in it: but it only works for those small enough to creep through the rocks — the rest of us have grown old and plump and forgotten innocence.'

He went away, noting the curse craft bobbing on the water and remembered the old stories. So people still came here to ill wish their enemies. There was sorrow in the thought. He bent and lifted a tiny cork with a flag on it from the water; saw the name and saw the cross above the evil, cancelling it out. Just removing it would not work, he thought. But this . . .

Hugh was watching him. He spoke softly.

'Father, forgive them for they know not what they do,' he said gravely.

Dai nodded. His people were foolish, were tattle tongued, were silly; but surely not evil, only misguided, never thinking about the words they spoke or the curses they made, hot with temper one moment and forgetting the next, and maybe some stole by night to remove the little craft from the water. Surely, too, there was no

70

truth in the old story for how could curses come by wishing?

He went to see Gwyn.

Gwyn wanted the bitch back. He would take the money for the pups. Thirty pounds each. That was nonsense, Dai said; with no breeding to speak of, for nobody knew the father of the puppies, not even Gwyn. Ten pounds each was more than enough, and if Gwyn thought otherwise there were one or two matters, like the hare in his kitchen right now, and the snare Dai had found on Gryff Evans land with a farm cat caught inside it, dead. Gryff had been very angry. He was fond of his cats.

'The RSPCA man now?' Dai said.

Gwyn said nothing, but next day went to the valley with a lead and chain in his hand, and waited till the bitch passed him. He grabbed her by the throat. She twisted and bit him, biting deep, biting in fear, hating the man who had chained her up and never fed her except with stale leavings from his own table.

He pulled out of her grasp and he went away, the bite hurting him, reminding him every moment of his hatred that was now an all-consuming passion, a desire to harm Hugh and Sula for thwarting him. But he would have to be cunning.

The pups were sold and Gryff and Dai were pleased with theirs; the others went to farmers beyond the valley who found them well reared and biddable. Gwyn received more money than he expected, for Hugh had paid for the bitch. He asked for a letter stating that she was not his, and under Dai's watchful eye, Gwyn wrote and signed it. His hand was bound in a dirty bandage. He did not want the brute back; she had bitten hard and might bite again. She too had been bewitched.

It would soon be bonfire night.

Every year the village built a large bonfire up on the cliffs. The children saved their pennies and bought fireworks; the mothers made their food for everyone, and on that night almost all the village except the babies and their mothers and the very old, were out enjoying themselves.

There was singing.

The bright coloured stars soared into the sky. Sula had shut the animals into the dark shed, where there were no windows, to keep them safe. The noise might bother them; the lights would frighten them more. She made a sleeping potion for them and put it in their food. She had shown Hugh more flowers in the forest that were good for healing. In her land they had a brief life and were carefully picked and her kitchen shelves were full of dried herbs and seeds and carefully preserved berries.

Gwyn watched her gathering them and knew even more certainly that she was a witch.

No children had brought wood to the cliff top at the end of the valley, but during the night the wood was shifted, into the valley, where, men said, it was more sheltered from the winds that always swept up from the sea.

It was a dark night, but fine. There were faint stars high in the heavens and a new young moon. The children wished and their elders turned their money.

The rockets soared into the sky.

Catherine wheels spun in mazy whirls of brilliant colour, the sparks falling to the ground.

Jumping jacks jumped and snapped and leaped and the children leaped and jumped and shouted.

The night was brilliant with light and noisy with sound that drowned the sighing of the sea on the shingle.

The bonfire blazed brilliantly, everyone adding

fuel, for all had brought wood. When the fireworks were gone there was singing and dancing, and then the children were taken home to bed and the young men cooked sausages and onions and baked potatoes in the ashes and the singing went on into the night.

No one noticed that the grass had caught fire; it was an odd fire, a single thin trail of flame, dancing soberly and quietly, almost unseen. Slowly along the valley, as if someone had laid a path for it. Moving ever onwards towards the cursing well; toward the little house that sheltered under the trees where Hugh and Sula and the animals slept peacefully. Wood was piled against the outer door.

The moon had set.

The stars were hidden in cloud.

A thin rain was falling.

Topsy, the bitch, woke and whimpered, smelling fire.

Hugh heard her, and went outside and saw the flame trail that came towards him. He filled a bucket and dowsed the ground all round the house. He walked along the path. A strange flame trail this, for the grass it burned was cut grass and dry straw laid on the path that led to his house. It had been laid by a human hand. For the first time Hugh was afraid.

He had not realized how they hated him.

He went inside and quieted the bitch.

Sula looked at him sleepily.

'What is wrong?'

He touched her dark hair with his finger, and pushed it back from her face. 'I am here and nothing is wrong,' he said.

She did not believe him.

In the morning she walked outside and saw the blackened grass; it led back to the bonfire. If Hugh had not wakened . . . but Topsy had protected them. She

73

had been named well. Hugh did not know why Sula had chosen her name; it seemed an odd one to him for a girl from overseas to choose. But Topsy in her tongue meant guardian. And Topsy had more than earned her name.

Sula felt safe when the bitch was at her heels. The seals followed, but they would not help her if anyone tried to harm her. Topsy would fly to her defence.

Gwyn saw how his plot had been foiled and anger mastered him.

This indeed was witchcraft for he had not lighted the trail until he knew they were asleep, the house quiet and dark under the midnight sky. She must have smelled the fire; fire calling to her, woman from the land of hell, of sulphur and of brimstone.

Gwyn's mind was twisting, becoming even more unbalanced, so great was his hate, and now he could believe in anything. In devils sent to torment him; in witches, sent to hound him, to steal his dog, to destroy his home. In his eyes his home had assumed grandeur, was a palace, and not a hovel that had not been cleaned for years. His horse now was stabled behind it, always at his call. The children sometimes heard him talking: 'Whoa now, steady there,' yet they saw no horse. They ran.

In the inn at night madness lent eloquence to his tongue, and the old men listened, charmed by the spate of words that tumbled from him. It was a long time since they had such talk. His angry mind coined words and phrases and gave him eloquence.

He spoke of the old magic that everyone had forgotten; the power of the standing stones; the power in trees; the power of the wind; the power of the sea. Power. Power of the storm, riding the hills; the power of the wind, savaging the mountains; the power of a woman sent from hell to mock and torment them; to bewitch Hugh into marriage. She was bringing more and more of her seal people here and one day they would assume human form and drive the villagers from their homes, and take over. They were the enemy.

The old men laughed, but listened and were uneasy.

It was nonsense, but could it, perhaps be true?

One night a sailor came to the inn, come from another town, to visit his sister and her husband; and his two nieces and to see the new baby. He had sailed all over the world, and had visited the island of North Uist, in the Outer Hebrides.

Here he had been told of the Clan MacCodum, known to those in the islands as Slioch nan Ron, the offspring of the seals. For long ago a seal woman had shed her skin and danced on the shore in the moonlight, fairer than any mortal and one of the islanders had seen her and been bewitched by her and had stolen her skin. He had hidden it so well she could not find it and she had married him and borne him sons, that looked to be human men, but all knew they were seal men. She had lived with him for many years and then, when near to death he had taken pity on her and brought her skin from its hiding-place.

It had been magically preserved, as fresh as the day she cast it and, just as the sun tipped the waves with light, she put it on again and behold, she was a seal again. He watched her swimming out of his sight, into the deep waters, somersaulting and flying up the waves, showing her joy, rejuvenated.

He was an old man, hobbling on two sticks.

Life held no savour when his wife had gone and soon he was taken to the graveyard and buried within sound of the sea, and it was said, every year on the anniversary of her going away, a lone seal came up from the water, and clambered to the grave and lay upon it, wailing.

It had happened, the sailor said. The people still spoke of it, and the men of the clan were all famous swimmers, more at home in the water than on land. No ordinary man could match them. And they were dark, their skins darker than most of the islanders, their hair sleek and blue black, their eyes brown as a seal's eyes and with the same doglike expression.

The sailor laughed as he talked, only half believing his own tale, until he was so well plied with beer that he would have believed the moon was made of hard boiled eggs and the bench he was sitting on had been carved from faery oak and had bewitched him for his speech had changed and he talked nonsense. He babbled of seals that turned into women all over the sea; of mermaids seen from his boat when the nights were long and dark and lonely; of seas that shone silver, sparkling eerily, fairy people flashing in their depths and coming to the surface to sing.

He remembered stories of long ago; of Circe bewitching the sailors, turning them all into pigs; and of the sirens; stories he had read merged with memory until he did not know truth from fiction. At last he slept, his head on his arms, while the old men nodded and spoke of more things in heaven and earth than men knew of.

One remembered one tale and one another and the talk took wings and flew.

Gwyn fanned it, a word here, a word there, until the fiery words followed one another fast and the stories grew to monstrous size.

Hugh was a wizard from the North and Sula the witch of Endor herself, in another guise, come to torment them, to destroy them.

9

Gwyn had dreamed great dreams of having power over other men.

Now at last he had it.

The power of words.

He stopped drinking even the tiniest sip of beer for beer fuddled his words as it fuddled the old men's wits, so that they listened to him greedily, laughing and nudging one another in the ribs and jeering; their beer-laden breath fanned his face as he bent towards them, telling them of yet more wickedness wrought by the witch woman.

For had not Gwyneth Evans lost her baby, born to breathe for only a few minutes, and that two days after the witch woman passed down the village street? And was not the cow at the end of the lane by the field beyond the cursing well barren for ever, never a calf, and now only fit for the knacker, a total loss?

And the twin lamb disease in the spring, the year before, which had started as the woman came ashore.

And old Bronwen at the farm under the mountain had died this summer too. Gwyn did not remind the old men that Bronwen was ninety-eight that year and had been ailing long before the seal woman came to the village.

'We are cursed,' he said his eyes glowing.

He was the man who saved the village from itself; he

was the man who brought them all to their senses, who told them of the evil in their midst, evil to which all but he had been blind.

Hugh was aware of more eyes that looked at him coldly; of men who crossed the street when he went to shop; of more women who spat at Sula, hands outstretched in the age old gesture that averted the evil eye. The village had gone crazy, he thought.

He preferred to walk the long trail over the hill to the village beyond the wishing well, while Sula came with him. But she was always aware of eyes on her whatever she did, yet she was never able to find them, for Gwyn was crafty and knew, as every poacher knows, how to take cover; how to hide his scent so that the dogs never caught a trace of him on the wind.

He had watched the pups grow. They were big and strong and bonny and he hated Sula even more, for the bitch too had altered beyond recognition. She had filled out so that she was twice her former size, and had a coat on her that would have won her prizes at any show, a glistening black and white coat that gleamed in the sun and stood, thick and sleek and beautiful, all over her body. He saw her daily. She ran to greet Sula joyously, her tail beating, her body weaving in ecstasy.

It needed little to fan the hatred; and this was much. Hatred choked him, growing to a monstrous size, disfiguring everything he saw. He thought of the curse on the slate, deep in the well, unseen, unblessed. He knew now that Hugh turned every curse back on itself by blessing the name of the one that was attacked; by adding the Christian cross, and the holy water; by praying to his own God to bring mercy and not malice on the head of the one that was named.

Deep winter was coming. There would be no more summer visitors to lighten the village mood. Few would venture far and they would grow in on themselves, alone at night in the houses, with dark brooding over them and the endless gales beating up from the sea.

The sea sang the winter dirge.

The wind howled the winter anthem.

There were few birds. Only the hunting owl, beating over the fields, creamy gold in colour, silent winged, dropping on unwary mole and mouse, bird of evil, bird of ill omen, bird that roosted by the cursing well, bird that Sula loved to watch, flying silently past, a ghostly bird of darkness, quiet under the lambent moon that shone nightly over the valley.

There were more seals now.

They came to hear the soft music that Sula played when the days were calm. Soon, when Christmas had come and gone and Easter was almost there, she would have a child. She longed for her own baby.

She sat on a rock on the beach, looking out over the water. Great ships passed on the horizon, and sometimes at night strange lights glowed above the water; glowed in the water; glowed under the water. And the moon shone and showed her a silver path that stretched into the distance, out of sight sliding over the far horizon.

Sometimes, as she thought of the future and the little son or daughter that might be hers, the ache for those long ago days of security was almost unbearable, and she lifted the reed pipe and played the soft lullabies that her holiday friends sang to the tiny babes that lay, kicking and laughing, in the hand-carved cradles.

The people loved to carve.

On long winter evenings they made animals as Hugh did; and little figures of men and women and children; they made tiny boats, and they made carved and ornamented boxes, and they carved the love symbols and the good luck symbols on the cradles they made for their children.

Sula drew a picture of her little brother's cradle; two solid ends, and lower solid sides, and two rockers so that a mother could calm a fretful teething child. For children were the same all the world over and mothers did the same things for them although not always in the same way.

Huge looked at the drawing and bought wood. Beautiful wood that was a joy to work, and he carved it strong and he carved it true. He did not carve pictures on the wood. He bought paints for Sula and she made the pictures for her child; pictures of her dreamland, and of the high icy hills and the goats and strange deer that roamed the icy plains; so that her baby would know from birth of the land where his mother had been so happy.

Gwyn had money for his pups and his bitch. He had money to spare to buy the men drinks; money to spend, so that they listened to him even more avidly when he told them of the cradle he had seen Hugh put outside the door; a cradle for a baby to be born to the seal woman. Another seal baby to add to those that roamed the big room as other people had children that played around in the evening.

It was not natural.

Three of the seals were grown; old enough to find a mate, and they went down to the beach and one day, did not come back. Hugh and Sula were sad and yet were glad, for they did not want to condemn their charges to a lifetime of captivity. Out there at night in the deep sea they would find their real home.

Little went well with the village.

They could not yet buy new pigs and the women envied Sula her skill with her needle, for they could not make such beautiful embroideries and sell them in the town. The men saw Hugh's little animals in the shops for a price far higher than he had been given and thought there must be money hidden in the little house by the well.

Much money.

One day Gwyn told them that Hugh and Sula had gone to the town. The house was empty, guarded only by the two collies. They would break in. The seals were harmless enough; seals did not fight.

The door was easy to force.

It was easy to smash everything in the two main rooms. The furniture and the ornaments; to slash the embroideries and the curtains, and the bright blouses. They had plenty of time. The dogs hurled themselves against the far door, shut in the room beyond.

The barking dogs guarded the big room, but Gwyn had poisoned meat in his pocket. He opened the door and held it out in his hand and his bitch saw him and rushed him, biting hard and deep and behind her the collie cur leaped for the second man, and charging rage came out of the room in the form of two little bull seals, their heavy bodies pushing and butting and teeth such as no dog ever boasted, biting deep. The poisoned meat dropped and lay wasted.

The men ran, and the animals went back to the big room, ignoring the food, waiting for Hugh and Sula.

That at least was undamaged.

They came home, laughing over their purchases, for they had been to buy wool and cloth to make more clothes for the baby. There would be beautiful clothes such as no one else had ever seen, for the babies in Sula's dreamland were cherished and everyone prepared for them; tiny embroidered garments bright with colour.

They opened the door.

There was nothing left whole. Everything they owned and loved was smashed beyond repair. The long nights of work were all wasted.

81

Sula was beyond tears.

She went into the big room. There was blood on the floor, but the animals were unharmed and came racing to greet them.

'They are safe,' Sula said. 'We can make new clothes and new furniture. We could not make new beasts.'

They went together to Dai the Police, and he came and looked and his anger grew. He went to see Gryff Evans, and Gryff came down to the little house.

'Come to me,' he said. 'My house is empty and I am a lonely man, and I have many rooms. And you will be safe there, for my dog will warn us of strangers, and there is room in the barns for the seals. You are not safe here.'

They did not want to leave the house by the well.

'Just until we find out who did this,' Gryff said. 'There is great evil; and you yourselves might be harmed.'

He helped them pack the things that were in the big room, and they loaded the seals and the dogs and the goat and the chickens and the few belongings that were left whole into his van. Dai helped them.

'We will come back,' Hugh said, as he closed the door. Behind the house the garden was as wrecked as the home had been; the bower destroyed, the vegetables planted for winter use were trampled flat.

That night in the inn Gwyn was triumphant, for they had driven away the evil. He did not know that they had moved in with Gryff.

'We will cleanse the place, and you will see, the evil will pass,' he said, knowing he would find the slate and remove it, and people would thank him for bringing prosperity back to the village. He, Gwyn would be important and respected, as he had always dreamed.

That night he rode his wild stallion along the cliffs until the moon vanished from the sky. He sang his triumph to the moon. Those who saw him saw only his swift sidelong sidle.

He knew now how to fan the fury of the old men and the very young; those who were middle-aged had more sense and were wiser, avoiding the group in which Gwyn was supreme. He bought drink to take out on to the cliff tops, and when the men were almost stupid with too much wine, he spoke of the witch woman.

'Fire cleanses,' he said, and watched with a grin on his face as the younger men took up the words.

Fire, fire, fire, was the chant.

They staggered down the cliff path, almost unable to stand erect, singing lustily.

Fire, fire, fire.

The little house was lined with wood.

It burned well and the wind fanned the flames, that grew to monstrous size.

High on the mountainside Hugh saw the fire, and looked down.

Gryff came to stand beside him, stony faced.

'It is a good thing you came to me,' he said.

'They would not have done it if we had been there,' Hugh said, but fear was mastering him. Sula slept. He did not wake her. He went out to the barn to make sure the animals were safe and Gryff came with him.

They sat at the kitchen table, looking down the valley.

'First my wife and little son,' Hugh said. 'And now this. What have I done to deserve such terrible things?'

'Nothing, my son,' Gryff said gently, feeling for Hugh as he felt for his own sons over the sea. Perhaps they would settle at the farmhouse and lighten his old age. It would be good to hear children's voices; to have the empty rooms filled with laughter, to have a woman around the place again. His wife's going had left it bleak and desolate.

But first they must deal with the village people, or he too would suffer. He had never known such evil among them. They were possessed, bewitched, their judgement clouded.

'Sula did not bring bad luck,' Hugh said.

'I know.'

'What can we do?' Hugh asked. 'We had better go, as far away as we can. But now, we have almost nothing . . . The baby must be safe.'

'We will see in the morning,' Gryff said, and Hugh went to his bed, to sleep at last and dream of fear; but he did not know what he feared.

Gryff sat all night, watching the road to his farm. No one could approach from behind, for there the mountain soared sharp and steep into the sky, a looming wall of barren rock that protected him from the winds that seared the hills. His young dog sat at his knee, aware of the need to watch, ears pricked, waiting. It was one of the collie pups. Outside in the yard the old dog listened too, and growled softly under her breath so that Gryff took his shotgun and went to see. Topsy and her son slept by Hugh's bed and growled too.

But it was only one of the tomcats coming home after visiting the village.

The wind was roaring again, blasting the trees, so that the animals huddled in the darkness, listening to the devils of the night.

So did the wind of evil roar through the village.

Gryff sat at the table and prayed, asking God to help him, for he was sure that men could not. No one had seen who wrecked the house; he knew that Gwyn must have talked them into it, but when the men went down in anger, Gwyn would not be there. He would be safe, with witnesses to show that he had nothing to do with it.

It was a long night and a cold grey dawn.

Sula woke, and looked out of the window towards the sea. Nothing was left of her home; only the black ashes of sorrow, marking the green grass which grew so thickly around it.

She stood for a long time, looking down at the ruins.

She went to feed the animals, and held the collie against her close, for comfort, shivering as she remembered. It reminded her of her own war-torn homeland. Gryff was still sitting at the table, his shotgun beside him. He was sound asleep. Sula stood the gun in the corner, first making sure it was unloaded. She began to cook and the smell of bacon and eggs woke the men.

'Sula,' Hugh said.

'I know.'

She dished the food, her eyes dark, her face stony, her thoughts withdrawn. She was not a woman who sorrowed aloud but the men knew that the hurt went deep.

'You are welcome here for ever,' Gryff said.

She look at him, startled.

'We cannot stay. It would not be safe for you. We bring sorrow with us, and those who would harm us will harm you.'

'I have lived my life and I will not tolerate evil,' Gryff said, anger in his voice. 'There is nowhere for you to go. You will always be different and those who do not understand will fear you. With me, you are safe, for I know your country and I know of your people and I know the dangers that you left behind you. I need help here. I am old and alone and afraid of dying with no one beside me. My children have forgotten me. I ask you to take pity on me and stay and we will face what there is to face together. You may be protected here. I belong to the valley. And when I go, there is the farm; none of my sons want it, and I gave them money long

85

ago so that I could leave it to someone who would cherish it as I have cherished it. Stay.'

Sula smiled at him. It was a sad smile that did not reach her eyes.

'My child will be born here if you wish,' she said. 'Thank you.'

It was a victory but as yet it led nowhere, for the village still hated them; and Gwyn was still free to rouse the old men and the young men; and there was the long winter with nothing to do and mischief to make.

Hugh looked at Gryff and they had no need of words.

That night Sula sat knitting, making a warm jersey for Gryff, by way of showing her thanks. The room was bright and clean, for she worked all day, and she cooked a meal for a king; and Gryff, sitting enjoying talk with Hugh, watching Sula's quick hands flash the knitting needles, looking at the dogs and the seals that had come indoors for company for a little while, thought how strange it was that out of great evil might come great good.

Perhaps they would prevail against the gossip-mongers and the mischief makers, and all would, in the end, be well.

But that night he and Hugh took it in turn to watch the valley and to watch for a telltale growl or an ear prick, lest men come with fire and anger and burn down this building also. Gryff put the beasts inside, in a big empty room that had once been a feed store, feeling that under one roof they were all safe.

But he could not keep his sheep safe.

In the morning there were six beasts lying dead inside the gate, with their throats cut.

They sent for Dai. But no one knew who had killed the sheep. Dai could do nothing.

10

The winter that year was one of the worst that men in the village could remember.

Gale succeeded gale, breeding out in the Atlantic, sweeping in over the hills, with snow and hail; with ice, and constant torrential rain.

Gwyn knew how to turn the floods to his advantage for now all knew that Sula would soon have a child. The rivers flooded; and receded. And flooded yet again.

'You will see when it is born,' he said. 'It will be a seal thing; perhaps half man, half seal; a monster, born to plague us. Her other sons are growing and she sends them back to the sea.'

The old men nodded wisely, but avoided one another's eyes, for even to them Gwyn's tales began to sound strange. Gryff and Hugh knew that total madness was not far away; that Gwyn was changing, and his twisted mind was becoming a crazed mind. The old men did not yet know. Nor some of the younger ones, who loved to hear Gwyn talk; to go away and think over his story of witchcraft; for the floods had brought idleness and there was nothing to do but talk.

Talk.

The words sped round the village, bred in houses and in shops; bred on street corners, flung into the air, some in jest and some in earnest, none quite the same as when they started. Whispers in ears; sidelong looks and glances and Sula no longer walked the village street, even with Hugh and Gryff, for she was deadly afraid.

Afraid of the glances that slid past her. Afraid of the women who crossed the street when she came by.

Afraid of the old men who glared at her with hatred in their eyes. Some of them muttered as she passed, an age-old protection rhyme against the Evil One, who, they were sure, was walking here in woman's guise. The woman from the sea who played with the seal pups as if they were her own babies; and who played her pipe by the water's edge and brought her brothers and her sisters to her. Sometimes they had seen her swim among them. Her dark hair on her dark head was seal like; she was supple and swift in the water, more than any woman they had ever seen. She dived and played with the waves, and she sang her strange uncanny songs, in her strange uncanny tongue.

Up in the farmhouse there was a kind of peace.

Never had it been so clean or so well cared for since Gryff's wife had died. Sula polished the furniture and washed the curtains; she scrubbed the floors and swept the hearths, glad to repay the old man for his kindness to them.

At night there was always a good meal on the table and Hugh and Gryff sat afterwards by the fire talking; Gryff remembering times when he was a boy, when people came from far and near to the Cursing Waters and the Wishing Well. Yet not all of them could reach the well, and wish.

Hugh carved a new cradle. This time Sula did not paint the sides; he carved them with tiny beasts and intricate flowers, putting all his heart into it to make up to her for the loss of everything that they had struggled for together.

Sometimes she sang to them.

She had learned the songs of Hugh's people, and she sang softly and low, and the seals listened and the dogs curled at her feet and the cats sat on her lap and the kittens nestled at her neck. Her hands worked baby clothes to replace those that were gone.

Sometimes they talked.

Gryff learned more of her dreamland; and they learned that her God and their God was the same God; a kindly God, a protector of the good people on earth, hoping always for the salvation of those that did evil.

He learned how when a child was born everyone came to bless it; bringing silver for wealth and an egg for long life and fertility; and salt to bless its bread; and a shell from the sea, because the sea was their living.

The women made clothes and embroidered them; and the men made a miniature canoe and a little spear, which were hung over the cot of a boy. If it were a girl child the women made a tiny doll that became the child's Luck charm, and that loss Sula regretted more than anything else for without her luck she had none; and was not that why so much anger was directed at her here? If only she had her luck doll again.

The rain stopped. Christmas was near.

The winds strengthened.

Roofs were torn away. Gardens were flattened. The winter crops were swept so fiercely that they were again flattened to the ground.

The sea began to invade the land, the wind piling the tides higher and yet higher, so that the waves surged against the cliffs and the cliffs weakened by the constant rain, fell on to the beaches and some of the village houses fell with them, though their occupants were saved.

It was the seal woman.

They must drive her away from the village.

They must make sure she and Hugh went far away and never came back.

Gwyn fanned the flames at night, enjoying his power. Power over men with words. He had never known such power. He had never known he could sway men to his will, could inflame them with passion, could make them senseless when they were sensible, could pick a word here, a hint there, a teasing suggestion there, and make them think that black was white and green was red and good was evil.

Gryff's gate was opened and all his stock led out. Men drove them along the road and left them milling senselessly. It took Hugh and Gryff the whole of two days to get them all back again. Gryff brought one of his billy goats down from the mountain.

He was nicknamed Savage and he deserved his name and kicked Gryff into the bushes twice on the way down. The next time men came creeping at night to release the stock Savage was by the gate; he butted the first man into the nettles; he butted the second man into the thistles and he butted the third man into the ditch. He was swift as a running deer and he was angry at such intrusion and he enjoyed butting people.

The field was left in peace after that.

Gwyn had new fodder for his fire for was not the goat the devil in disguise, and had not the seal witch called on him to protect Gryff's stock? And was not Gryff, who was a godly man, bewitched himself that he should offer a home to a witch and devil brood?

The remaining seals now followed Sula about the farm.

She fed them and they loved her for it, and were always hoping that she might be bringing food for them, even when it was not feeding time.

She thought of her baby and was afraid; for the villagers were cruel to her and how would a child live here among people who hated him? She crept away one day, shutting the seals and the dogs in the barn, going hesitantly down the cliff path, her eyes watchful, afraid she might meet Gwyn, yet not wanting Gryff or Hugh to know her destination.

The tunnel was narrow but not yet too narrow for her. She crept along it, and came out into the valley. Winter had hold here, but it was a kind hold for no wind came down the pass. The sky was clear and the deer grazed by the water, lifting wise-eyed heads and looking at her. There was a hare, washing its face like a cat.

She knelt by the wishing well, looking into the deep pure waters.

She cupped her hands and drank.

She asked for freedom from fear for Hugh; for acceptance by the villagers, for gentleness for her child; for freedom to remain with Gryff, for now they both loved the old man. He was lonely for company, missing his sons and daughter, missing his wife, with no one to care for him if he were ill. There was no one for him to talk to in the long silent evenings except for the dogs and the cats who came indoors to keep him from the desolation of a house where nothing moved except himself.

Slowly peace returned to her. She lay quietly on the grass, and slept. The deer cropped all around her, unafraid. A fawn came to look at her, and she opened her eyes to see him gazing down at her, astonished, never having seen a human before.

It was an age-old holy place; a place of beauty. There was nothing to disturb the calm.

There was a promise in the still air, an echo of a ghost voice from long ago when the world was young and kinder, when the beasts only ruled here, and man was yet in the future; the birds sang of promise; of a time when she would know happiness again as she had known it in her own land.

She could not stay by the well.

Peace was an interval between times of trouble, a rare moment in a long life that was forever prey to anxiety; to fear. She walked back to the farm, knowing there were eyes watching her, knowing that Gwyn hated her. Yet she could never see him. He was secret and hidden as the wild deer themselves, but far more dangerous than even the big stags in the rutting season when they roared their challenges across the forests.

Her child would soon be born.

And now she was afraid for him.

He would grow up in a strange land, a land where he and she would always be strangers; not accepted by the people; and even children had cruel tongues. He would be an alien, teased and tormented, bullied and hated, as she was hated. And there might be worse.

She thought of the six dead sheep and shivered, and that night Hugh and Gryff watched her helplessly as she sat closer and closer to the blazing woodfire and could not get warm. She had withdrawn into her own loneliness and though she made their food, and cleaned the farm, she was quiet as the dogs that followed at her heels. They, sensing her unhappiness, tried to console her with cold noses pushed roughly into her hand, trying to distract her and bring her out of the dark world she had gone to, into the everyday world where dogs played and seals romped and people laughed.

There was no more laughter.

Only fear.

Gryff knew fear now too, for the village had been tainted by evil, had been destroyed by stupidity, had been provoked to a madness such as he had never known. Hugh knew fear; he was afraid that Sula might leave him, might one day swim out into the cold sea from which she had come and he would never see her again. His own people were too cruel.

Gryff watched them both.

And one night he wrote a letter.

He needed help.

11

Bill Harrison could not forget the village or the girl they said was a seal. He knew the story to be absurd, but he knew also that the old men half believed it and that the women, jealous of her, would like to believe it too.

He read Gryff's letter with growing unease.

He read of the dead sheep, and of other small incidents that were building up in to a story that might have a very ugly ending.

Yet surely people like that did not live today.

People did not change.

Their manners might change and their clothes might change; they might use machines where once they used horses and ridden in carts, but they were the same as ever; wayward, foolish, afraid of the dark and the unknown, believing in magic and witchcraft and ghosts; with the long ago race memories still important to them. Nothing they learned in school could rub those out.

Bill had been born wanting to know. His family called him the elephant's child because the elephant's child had always asked WHY? Why was the sun hot and the moon cold? Why were the nights dark and the days bright? Why did some men like beards and others go bare faced? Why was a dog a dog and a fish a fish? Many adults thought his questions stupid, but he knew what he wanted to know.

It made him a good reporter.

He was just starting a week's holiday.

He did not know how he could help, or what he could do. He cancelled his plans and drove down the motorway and turned into the narrow hedge-lined roads that wound and twisted along the sides of the mountains.

He drove through dark forests where snow lay on the trees.

He drove past small villages where the children came to watch him pass.

So little happened in their world.

He drove through the village. People watched him, recognizing his car, knowing he was bound for the farm where Hugh and Sula now lived with Gryff. They did not want anyone else there. Gwyn had plans; a stranger might spoil them. But the man was slight; no match for some of the villagers; and there were many of them.

The women waited.

The child would soon be born.

A witch child, a seal child, a seal pup; it must be born looking like a seal and then, would it change, or were the other pups her pups too; this woman from the sea who swam with the seals and talked with the seals and brought the seals running when she sang.

It would be a devil child and if the mother brought so much evil, what would the child bring?

They asked one another and they forgot kindness and laughter. The heavy brooding fear lay over all of them as the time for the birth came nearer.

The midwife; would she go to the house of wickedness for surely now Gryff was as wicked as they? He no longer came to preach in the church; surely God would reach down and touch him with death, or with

95

silence . . . he would be punished for harbouring the followers of the Evil One.

Time was passing and Sula was now a shadow in the house, even her busy fingers still. She was afraid to go out alone, for if she did, Gwyn followed her. She did not see him, but she knew he was there and if the dogs were with her they walked beside her, hackles roused, growling angrily under their breath, ready to dart out and bite if she gave the command. But she could never give such a command.

The days passed.

Snow blocked the road out of the village. The people were cold. Ice formed on the streams, and Sula saw a world daily that looked more and more like her dreamland and the sickness in her grew. She wanted to go back. Back where there was laughter and friends and her mother to talk with and the girls she knew who would make clothes for her child. If only she could go and take Hugh with her. There was no war in her dreamland.

But they had no money for the journey. She was lonely too because she had not mastered Hugh's language. She was as helpless as the dogs when it came to trying to make him understand some of the thoughts and feelings in her head, for there were no ways to show feelings. How did you explain sorrow in words in an alien tongue; or fear? or happiness? Gryff and Hugh only knew that she was sad, and that the sadness in her was now almost an illness and they did not know what to do.

The village doctor prescribed a tonic. He did not know of the gossip. No one dared tell him.

Sula did not need tonics. She needed friends to laugh with; she needed women's talk; she needed to know where she could buy things for her coming child;

and how to care for it, for that she did not know.

Hugh and Gryff were kind but they could not know how she felt.

At night she lay wakeful, looking from the window to the snow-covered hills and pretended that she was at home, her mother in the next room, and in the morning they would talk together, and choose a name for this child of hers, a name worthy of him, for he would grow to be a brave man, like his father, but also like her brother. Perhaps she would name him for her brother. Perhaps that would ease her grief. She had never missed them so much.

When she slept, she cried out and there was no way that Hugh could comfort her.

12

The snow melted.

February gave way to March and March to April and it was time for Sula's child to be born.

The village waited, for Gwyn had said she would give birth, not to a human baby, but to a seal; and they must steal the child before evil came to them. He would seem to them human, but at night Sula and he would don their sealskin garments and go down to the sea and call to her sisters, and even greater evil would come to the village.

The cliffs were crumbling and the houses would slide into the sea.

The sea would break into the land and that would be the seals doing for they wanted the places that men used. They wanted to rule the world, and they would do so, for they were able to take on human shape.

The madness in Gwyn was showing more daily, but the old men, half asleep, halfway to dying, not heeding words too well or hearing words too well, sat and nodded into the beer mugs, old eyes wrinkled and hooded, old hands gnarled and bent. They were aware of little that went on in the world today, though all could remember childhood and long fair days and hours spent fishing — the first tiddlers caught and frogspawn in the spring — and the taste of a birthday dinner, and the sweetness of those long-ago ices and cakes, far better than any food cooked today.

The village people lived their lives indoors; they watched, nightly, the babble of voices from the television sets — death seemed to come in a thousand different guises; death from drowning, from knife, or bullet, from car accidents, from a murderer walking slyly through the dark. It was as if, in their search for life, death had become the only reality and they watched it avidly.

Sula had watched the set in Gryff's sitting-room; and with Hugh and Gryff had removed it to another room. They spent the nights in quietness round the fire, the men talking over the day; the lambs in the field and the time of the next shearing, the young bull calf born that day; the milk from the goats, and the kid due soon.

Sula listened. She moved wearily, and no longer sang as she worked in the house.

The world was as grey and wicked as the grey stories of misery and wrath that had once been shown in the corner of the room.

Sometimes they went to watch on the screen, the world of animals; of foxes, living their secret lives, doing little harm to others; of hawks, diving through the air, of owls, winging over the fields; of tropical beasts in lands ravaged by the sun. It was hard to believe there was a sun on the grey days that seemed to have come to stay in the valley.

The slow days passed.

Hugh visited the town and brought back toys for the baby; and all the other essentials, having asked the chemist what he would need. The farm was quiet when he returned. Gryff was busy and Sula sat watching the flames in the fire, as if they would conjure up for her all that she lacked. She no longer smiled to greet him. There was a great fear over her that she could not dispel; a fear that harm would come to her child.

Gwyn no longer hid.

He walked past the farm, his sideways movements more apparent, his sideways smile crooked on his face, giving him an expression more evil than when he did not smile. He looked in at the windows from the road, but how could they move him, for he was outside their land and he had a right to walk the roads. He led a charmed life, for his wild horse could soar into the clouds when danger threatened. That he knew.

Sometimes there were others with him.

They stood, watching.

Sula kept the curtains drawn and the room darkened. She kept the dogs by her.

Gryff loaded his shot gun night after night, saying nothing to Hugh, but Hugh knew. Bill now watched with them, having caught their fear.

None of the men slept.

Nor did Sula.

She listened to the wind that sighed beyond her windows and the sound of footsteps was always in her ears. Were they walking there, outside in the dark? Or were they haunting her, the long-ago people who farmed here? Her people believed in ghosts; in the souls of the dead come back to earth to expiate their past crimes, and even their small sins. They believed in angels who would help them in their need, so she prayed often, to her own guardian angel, but it seemed that she had left him behind in her childhood country and he did not know where to find her.

He had deserted her family when guerillas took over her own land.

She spent time with the seals, playing with them and watching them play with the dogs. They did not condemn her or criticize her, or make her feel alien. They loved her and butted her hands and asked for her to stroke them. And with them she was always at peace.

100

They loved her more than ever and followed her every-where, a strange little procession that Gwyn saw and reported on, embroidering the story at night. He told how she spoke to them in their own language and they answered her, and how he had seen her swim with them even when ice was on the rivers and snow on the hills. And how he knew the big chest in her bedroom, the hope chest of all the brides that had ever come to the farm, holding their new trousseau and their fine linen and beautiful embroidered clothes, held only her sealskin. And soon would hold the child's for he would be born in it.

Gwyn thought now only of the child.

The night it was born they would cleanse the village, by fire, by destruction, and would punish Hugh for wedding the witch and Gryff for harbouring the witch.

Gwyn made a bomb.

He liked the thought of a bomb.

Fire was quiet.

Matches brought only a whisper, a hiss of sound.

A bomb, big, splendid, going off with the noise of a thousand fire crackers; now that was something to con-sider. He would be a man to be respected, a terrorist chief, a man who had made a bigger and better noise than any in the village.

He knew where to steal what he needed.

He knew how to make what he needed.

He spent his evenings indoors now, not going near the inn. The men wondered — and began to think again, for themselves, away from the foul tongue that spun them lies in a tone like silver.

Gwyn knew they would forget so he went back to the inn and told them once more of Sula singing to her seals; and how she was followed by the little menagerie. He told of the reporter who stayed there with the farmer Gryff, who was now tainted with the same evil.

Evil.

Witchcraft and a witch baby.

A cow died at the end of the village, and Gwyn said Sula had passed only two days before. Then the children began to get the mumps, and he said Sula had touched one of the children only days before, holding a hand against the baby's cheek. The mother snatched it back into the house but not soon enough.

The child was ill by the end of the week.

The time came.

Sula's son was born just as the sun came over the mountains. The district nurse was with her, and the doctor. A fine boy. Sula looked at him, but her sorrow did not lift.

Outside the farmhouse Gwyn waited, until he heard the first cries of a newborn child and then he hurled his bomb, flinging it into the haystack, where it exploded and the rich red flames rioted in the hay.

Cats and dogs ran and cattle lowed and sheep bleated.

Gryff took his gun and ran. The villagers, seeing the flames, were suddenly appalled; the men came with hoses and water to dowse the fire. Gwyn had gone to find the curse slate in the well, to finish his work. He did not see the shamefaced men, horrified and shocked to sanity, fighting bravely to keep the fire from the farmhouse where Sula lay sleeping, exhausted after the birth, her son in her arms, knowing nothing of the holocaust beyond the windows. The nurse stayed with her. No one had ever dared tell the stories of the seal woman to her. Bronwen had an angry tongue and a way of making people feel ashamed at their evil thoughts. Nor did the doctor know, for he too would have scoffed at them and told them to go home and pray to be forgiven for their wickedness. Dai the Policeman came to help. He had never been so angry in his life. He hated the villagers.

Morning came.

Weary men, smoke sore and blackened faces, sat at the kitchen table drinking tea. The hope chest was in the corner of the room, and their eyes sought it, wondering what was inside. The nurse came out and opened it, revealing shawls and little dresses, the work of the long evenings and Sula's busy hands. She took out what she needed and showed it to them.

'Isn't it beautiful,' she said.

She brought the child to them, washed and clean and dressed in fragile clothes made by his mother. His dark hair lay like a cap against his head. He opened blue eyes to look at them; Hugh's eyes. He made a small fist with his tiny hand.

The morning dawned clear, a blue sky and a hot sun, the first warm sun of the year.

Bill was glad that he had come to the farm. He had worked harder than anyone, putting out the fire, his thoughts racing. Now he had a plan, but he told no one, not even Hugh.

By day the men had gone to their work, and the only sign of trouble was the burnt out stack. Everyone had worked to tidy the place, and the women stayed on.

Sula lay in her bed.

The women had come to see her child and brought gifts for him, now bitterly ashamed of their thoughts.

The wind died.

The sun shone brightly and dried the overflowing waters from the fields. The oppression lifted from the village.

The child had brought them luck.

Bill had a surprise, too.

He had looked at Sula's pictures and had talked to her, learning of her long-ago holiday in the country of ice and snow; of her happiness there, and because he found it easier to teach her than did Hugh, he learned too of her own country. He showed it to her on the map and her pointing finger revealed what he had guessed.

She came from a country where men fought bitterly still; where guns and bombs were part of the daily scene and there was no justice.

'I will never go back,' she had said. 'But sometimes I wish we had stayed in my childhood holiday place; there the people are so good.'

She had drawn her luck doll for him.

'Hugh must make one for our son,' she said.

She had always been sure she would have a son.

Bill listened to the women talking. He helped Gryff clear the burnt straw. He mended the broken gate. They found the pieces of the bomb and showed them to Dai.

Bill had seen Gwyn throw the bomb.

The man had been outlined against the sky as the flames flashed into life.

Bill stood at the gateway, willing Evans the Post to come in his little red van. The van struggled up the path. The field to the farm was rutted and hilly; rock outcrop threatened the exhaust of the van and Evans climbed out.

'A parcel from Hull,' he said.

He looked at the burnt out stack and shook his head sadly.

'Such wickedness. What gets into people?' he asked. He had never been among the gossips, and nor had his wife, though his son had come home once from the Vaults and told him what was being said and been forbidden to go there again.

Gwyn had been seen on the cliffs, watching the farmhouse and singing. Wild songs of hate that had startled his hearers.

Bill took the parcel indoors and handed it to Sula.

'A gift for your son,' he said.

She smiled at him and opened it, and then lay for a long time, unable to speak.

The little luck doll lay in her hands, a tiny doll, a toy doll with blue eyes and black hair, and dressed in thick furs; it held a toy spear in one hand and a tiny canoe in the other.

'We will hang it on the wall above his cradle,' she said, and when the women brought her food she showed it to them.

'It will bring good fortune to everyone,' she promised.

They could not do enough.

They brought flowers for the rooms and cleaned the farmhouse; they brought presents for the baby. Eggs for long life and silver for wealth; one brought a tiny crucifix of silver to hang around his neck; others brought sweets for Sula, and fruit, and home-baked bread. They could not make up for all that had passed.

The seals fretted and the dogs fretted, so Sula was helped into the big sitting-room to lie where the beasts could see her. She petted them and showed them her son.

They sniffed at him, gently, and knew that here was another creature come to live with them and be cherished.

The wind had gone and the sun shone bright, and the old men could not understand what happened to them.

Bill and Dai spoke together, and when no one was watching, they went off in Bill's old car.

They asked for news of Gwyn, but no one knew of him.

He had vanished.

Bill had to return to his work.

Dai went on looking and listening.

And one day a boy came with news.

Gwyn was living in a cave down on the beach and at night he still ran on the cliffs and shouted his wild songs to the stars, but now there was a madness in them that even the boys recognized, and they were afraid as they had never been afraid before.

Now they knew where evil lay.

There was a devil living inside Gwyn, and the man haunted the cliffs.

Hugh, who still watched over the cursing well, found the curse crafts there daily; cursing every man in the village, every woman and every child, and he spent his time grabbing them and writing the sign of the cross above them. The minister, the vicar and the priest from the nearby town came to try and bless the well, and end the evil.

It would be covered and the cover locked, but it took time to make the cover. The well was an odd shape, and the water from it trickled out in a thousand tiny springs.

Hugh did not know that the slate that had caused all the trouble lay at the bottom.

Trouble still came to the village for craziness had brought Gwyn cunning.

Here was a shed burned down; Gwyn loved fire and the flames that flared into the sky.

A child lost his bicycle, and it was found thrown into a pool on the shore, flung from the cliffs to break on the rocks below.

The hens' eggs vanished.

Foxes were seen where no fox had been seen before. Gwyn snared them and released them to prey on the chickens.

The village had not listened to him.

Now they would all suffer.

At night he rode his white stallion and trampled the

ground with its hooves; calling to it to punish the men who rejected him.

Those who saw him running sidelong, leaping crazily, crossed themselves or prayed to their God to deliver them from evil. It was impossible to catch Gwyn.

He knew paths that no other man knew.

He knew how to melt into the shadows; and when to be silent as the hunting fox. He knew where to find food; from the pools and from the old garden that Hugh no longer tended but where vegetables still grew among the weeds.

He had water and he stole milk from the grazing cows, milking them swiftly and secretly into the can he had fetched from his hut.

Only at night did he run free; riding for ever, on the horse that only he knew existed.

He went at night stealthily to the hills above Gryff's farm.

He opened the gates, and the sheep and cattle strayed.

When the gates were all padlocked, he made holes in the walls, taking the stones down one by one, leaving gaps big enough to release the beasts.

Gryff brought all his billy goats down; they protected the sheep and the cattle, charging through the darkness at Gwyn, scenting him from a distance. They dared not leave the dogs out, lest he carried poisoned meat.

He must be found, Dai said.

But that was easier said than done.

They found his cave, but he had moved by then and hid in a ruined cottage on the moors. Sometimes he slipped back to his hut and switched on his television set, very softly, lest anyone pass and hear, sitting crouched in the darkness, the windows blocked so that no light should shine from the set.

Up on the moors, he caught partridges; and pheasants and fed well.

He made stews, with vegetables stolen from the village.

He broke the walls of all the farms around.

He must be stopped, Dai said again.

The villagers who once had listened to him now hated him. He stole their tools and he stole from their gardens; he took what he wanted when he wanted, yet nobody saw him. He knew who had dogs and who had not. No warning bark alerted anyone.

Most of all, he wanted to harm Sula.

Because of her, the village had turned against him. It was she who brought bad luck, not he. If she had never come he would never have cursed the place.

The curse was lasting.

Gwyn was a plague all by himself.

He hid on the hills and watched a storm break over the village.

Lightning flash and fire fear.

Fire.

He loved fire, and from that time began to use fire to do his bidding. They would learn who was master.

They would fear him as they never had feared him before.

He fired the stacks and there was no winter fodder for the animals.

He fired three hedges and he burned down a garage up on the top of the hill.

The firemen were kept busy, day and night, never knowing where Gwyn would turn up next, no one ever seeing him, or hearing him.

Now he did not sing on the cliffs, lest anyone heard him.

He lay in the cottage and talked to his horse.

'You and I together; we will trample the fields of growing corn; we will run through the wheat and run through the barley; we will fire the stacks and fire the thatch; we will spoil, you and I together, my fine beauty.'

And he would hear the horse neigh in reply. And reach out a hand to stroke its fiery muzzle, and see it standing by the stone wall, dipping its head to his hand.

Some nights it did not come.

Then he was frightened, wondering if it had deserted him. Those were the nights that the poachers loved when the moon hid her face and blackness was absolute, and no man could move without a light.

When the moon rode high his horse returned to him.

Then he longed to hide on the cliffs and sing his war songs.

One he loved above all. He had learned it in school.

'We are they who come swifter than Fate,
We are they who rise early or late;
We storm at your ivory gate.
Ye Kings of the Sunset, beware.'

He could not remember it all.

'The sun or the moon for a lamp and the swing of the wind in our hair.'

The voice of the wind.

It now spoke to him as often as his horse spoke.

It told him to watch Gryff's farm, where Hugh and Gryff watched over the baby, now growing, now crawling, now almost older than the standing corn.

And it was then, when harvest was near and the village had relaxed, that the winds came, and showed Gwyn how to get his revenge.

Night after night men found their crops had been trampled, by what seemed like a crazy animal, rushing up and down the fields, flattening the barley, pushing down the wheat, scattering the rye, scything parts of it here and there, making it impossible for the combines to reap.

Gryff suffered most of all.

His walls were torn down nightly; his beasts released and for ever needing to be rounded up. The foxes got into his chickens having apparently cut the wire.

The water in his well turned blue overnight, so that daily he and Hugh had to fetch fresh water. Sula stayed close by the house and her child, and watched the dogs and seals, and grew thin with watching. Hugh grew angrier as each day went by and they could never find Gwyn, though all now knew that he was the source of their trouble.

The water in the cattle troughs turned blue.

The big ram turned blue overnight, having been sprayed from the wrong side of the wall, with paint that would not come off him.

Gwyn had moved his home again.

Now he slept in a deserted farmhouse, in luxury, for it had belonged to an old lady who had died. No one could find her heirs, so all the furniture was still there, and the kitchen was filled with tinned food.

He fed like a lord and rested and dreamed of his winter ploys.

The village would be sorry they had refused to listen to him.

The witch woman and her brat were still there in the farmhouse.

There were pigs in the village again.

He planned a way to destroy them. Pigs were the village prosperity. Somehow he would poison all the swill; and the pigs would die and they would blame the seal woman.

He saw her now daily in the waves, watching him.

They didn't know she was the big seal in the cove, but he knew.

He knew everything.

When the waves roared he let his wild laughter mix with their noise. When the wind roared, he galloped endlessly on the night-time sand, and the waves washed away all trace before morning.

13

Fire . . . Gwyn loved fire.

He loved the lightning flash in the thunder sky,
when the flickering glows tore through the clouds;
when the fireballs floated and hit the trees, when the
world crashed and roared and shouted for him, for he
could never hope to make such a wonderful noise.

He slipped through the bushes and watched the
farm.

Sula knew he was there; she felt the hate of him
although she never saw him.

The collie bitch knew he was there. She smelled the
hate of him although she never saw him.

When she turned her head, her eyes searching the
bushes, her teeth bared in a silent snarl. Sula picked up
her child and ran indoors.

The witch and her witch child.

The villagers were fools. Only Gwyn knew that the
witch woman swam in the waters now daily, watching
him, her great eyes brooding, dreaming up spells.

It was her wiles that meant he must hide like a wild
animal, and avoid the villagers. She had taught them
well. Taught the children to run if they saw him;
taught the women to race indoors and shut the curtains
so that he could not see; taught the old men to avoid
him.

Sometimes her son swam with her.

He saw them both in the water, and he saw more, for he now knew that she could be in two places at once. He had watched her swimming with the pups beside her, and then turned his head and seen her on the cliffs walking with her child in a carrier on her back, such as none of the village women used.

He turned his head and there she was in the sea, the black domed head watching him; the pup's head raised inquisitively too.

Yet again when he looked she was on the cliffs, making towards Gryff's farmhouse. She had been visiting with her son and was coming home through the dusk, for the village thought that Gwyn had gone away.

He had not tormented them for two weeks.

Gwyn had been galloping on the midnight sands when clouds hid the moon.

He slipped on the rocks and fell.

His ankle twisted. His foot swelled, and was black and blue and yellow and maddened with pain; all his madness festered in his foot. He had to stay quiet as it would not bear his weight, and while he stayed, he brooded.

He would kill the witch woman.

He would return her child to the sea.

He would fire the village and punish them for their rejection.

The moon no longer shone at night.

Rain came from overwhelming clouds.

Rain that flattened the corn and the wheat and the barley.

Rain that spoiled the harvests.

Rain that would not let Gwyn's fires take hold.

The swelling eased.

The pain went from his foot and returned to his head, increasing in intensity.

113

He managed, one night, to hobble to his old hut. No one ever came near. They all thought he had gone. He let himself inside and crouched down in the dirty room, and gave himself up to the wonders of his magic box that told stories and showed him pictures such as men a century ago had never dreamed of.

The story they told was of a man who burned down a village, using a bomb. Smoke and flame rioted across the screen and Gwyn hugged himself in delight. Yellow sweeping fire; fire red, fire gold, fire flicker, fire glow, demon fire, devouring, dragon fire, belching from the mouths of monsters, fire cold and fire hot, hellfire burning.

The clouds had gone from the moon.

He came out when the village lay sleeping, on to the cliff tops and the bright beams poured over the water; the round moon shone down on him.

Hunter's moon.

Witch's moon.

Devil moon.

Fire moon.

He would burn down the village with the biggest bomb man ever made.

He would steal the witch's child and throw it from the cliff tops, down on to the rocks, down into the deep sea.

Then the village would welcome him home.

Then they would respect him and fear him because of the power in his hands.

The power in his mind.

The power of his wild white horse.

He patted it and let it go and watched it soar into the sky. Tonight he had kept it earth bound. Tonight he had galloped across the sands.

The fishermen who came to the beach in the morning saw the tide had not yet washed away Gwyn's footsteps.

They looked at the marks of his shoes, here, there, everywhere, and one of them went to warn Dai that Gwyn was back.

Gwyn was back.

There might be fire again.

Gryff looked to his gates and his walls, and moved his sheep and cattle into fields close to the house, and put the goats among them.

At night the village bolted and barred all doors. The children were not allowed to play in the streets. The old men moved uneasily, glancing over their shoulders into the shadows. The young men moved as if they were hunting.

Dai asked a colleague to come and bring his police dog.

Gwyn knew all about dogs.

He was hidden in the bushes watching Sula when the dog came.

He slipped away, into the cliff tunnels, where scent was flung wildly by eddies and currents of air. There was an old shaft that went to the beach, a shaft from long ago when men smuggled and the packhorses came to the shaft head, taking the laces, brandy and wines that came from France.

There was a steep ladder, falling away into the ground, down into a cave that led to the beach. Men had sent their goods up here by long ropes. Gwyn had tied a rope to the top of the ladder to give him extra handholds, and now he slipped down the rope, not caring about his hands, to get away from the dog.

They found nothing. Not a trace of him anywhere.

Hugh went down to the cursing well and found new curses daily.

Gwyn cursed the village.

He cursed Hugh and Gryff and Sula.

And then, one day, he cursed the baby.

Hugh looked at the curse and wrote the sign of the cross and stopped to pray and after that the baby was never left alone. Sula watched over him and Hugh watched over him and when Bill came he too watched, catching the village unease.

Gwyn began to fire the mountain.

Here a fire, there a fire, here a trail of smoke and there a plume of smoke.

There were matches in the deserted farmhouse.

There were voices now that told him what to do. Voices in the night from his horse, that had eyes like burning stars and ears like a sickle moon, and a plumed tail that flowed in the wind and anger in his punishing hooves.

Gallop when the wind was high.

Gallop when the waters raged.

Gallop through the night, stopping here and stopping there to light a little fire, to burn a little tree, to burn the bushes, to burn the moors, to burn the heather.

Fire in the woods.

Fire in the straw.

Fire on the hedges.

Fire in the heather.

Not too close to the village at first.

He would show them.

Dai spoke to the village men in the Vaults one evening.

'Gwyn must be stopped.'

'But how?'

They could not shoot him as they would shoot a mad dog among the sheep. He was, after all, a man.

They could only watch and wait, and try and guess what he would try to burn next; where he would appear next. And keep the women and children safe, for it was obvious to all now that madness had overtaken Gwyn and he needed to be caught before disaster came to them all.

The fires eased some of the anger.

Never enough.

He had to kill the witch and save the villagers. Witches needed silver bullets. He needed silver.

There was a silver horse in the farmhouse where he now lived all the time. No one ever came there.

He melted it down in a pan and made two bullets. A big one for the woman; a small one for the child.

He had no gun but he could use a catapult as he used it on the pheasants and the partridges.

He would lie in wait.

He would also make a bomb.

No bomb made of gunpowder would do for Gwyn.

It would be a witch bomb, carrying hate; a bomb that would fire the whole village and fire the woods and the fields and burn down the mountain.

Such a bomb had never been made.

He had to pick the right herbs at the full of the moon.

He knew the herbs he needed.

Put together they would make such a fire as had never been seen on earth.

Achilles millefolia for war.

Anemone for sickness.

Aspen for lamentation.

Basil for hatred.

Begonia for dark thoughts.

Bilberry for treachery.

Birdsfoot trefoil for revenge.

Coltsfoot to assure that justice was done.

Coronella for success to crown his wishes.

Creeping cereus for horror.

Cypress for death.

Dragonwort for evil.

Fleur de lis and fleur de luce for flame and fire.
Enchanter's nightshade for witchcraft.
Harebell for grief.
Imperial Montague for power.
Mandrake for terror.
Marigold for despair.
Whin for anger.

There were other plants that he could add; witch's blood, devil's bit and devil's foot, and snakebit; woundwort and baneberry; bitter cress and hemlock; spleenwort and lousewort; pepperwort and scurvy grass; wormwood and broomrape. He would mix and mash them together, and bind them together and put them in a pig's bladder; and set light to it and hurl it among the little cottages with thatched roofs at the far end of the village.

The village would burn.

When he closed his eyes he saw the glory of the fire; the rising flames, the billowing smoke and he heard the cries of the people.

He would stand above them, and when they begged for mercy he would laugh at them, and his laughter would thunder in the hills.

He had to wait for a stormy night.

He had to pick at the full of the moon.

It was not easy to find the plants; leaves of some and roots of some and some in flower.

He hunted night after night, forgetting to ride his white horse.

Though it walked beside him and spoke to him.

It grazed beside him, feeding on Yorkshire Fog and Panic Grass and feverfew; on witch's vetch and dragonsbit and deadly nightshade.

On poison plants that gave it strength so that when it lifted its head and neighed the neighs resounded from the mountain behind the village like thunder on the hill, and Gwyn lifted his head and yelled above the neighs.

'Heigh, heigh, heigh, heigh,' and the sounds re-echoed.

The village shivered.

The noise came thinly, like the call of a searching owl, like the banshee scream of a lost ghost, haunting the moor.

It did not sound human.

Gwyn made his bomb.

He made his bullets.

He hunted the farmhouse and found elastic in the old woman's unneeded clothing.

The moon had been full and had slipped away to nothing and fed and fattened and was full again.

Witch's moon.

Devil's moon.

Moon to light him, moon to show him where to throw the bomb.

He stood on the mountain looking down on a toy village; toy men and toy women and toy children crawled the streets.

He was a god.

They would thank him for ridding them of the witch and her pup.

Soon.

Below him Sula spent the days happily with Hugh and Gryff and her baby. The women visited her and she visited them. She showed them how to embroider the flowers and trees that grew around them, and how to make pictures on cloth. And they showed her how to make *bara brydd* and crisp crusty bread, and cake that melted in the mouth.

The baby grew and played with other babies.

The collies protected him, herding him from danger as if he were a small and adventurous lamb, keeping

119

him from falling in the midden or going too near the pigs.

Bill visited every weekend, glad to be away from the uncomfortable lodging he had in the town. He liked to sit and talk and laugh with Gryff and Hugh and Sula, where the fire glowed and the room was bright with vivid flowers and yellow curtains, and shining silver and brass.

Gryff had not been so happy since his wife died.

The baby made them all laugh as he explored his world and found it good.

He learned to crawl, and he learned a few words and he learned to stand.

Yet always there was fear behind the laughter, and when Gwyn's wild yells sounded on the mountain, the curtains were drawn close, the doors bolted, and the men had water and sand ready, in case of fire.

They went to hunt him, and he was never there. He moved like a shadow for all his sideways creeping walk; he ran like a deer, for all his twisted legs. He moved sometimes in a strange gallop, like a child playing at horses, but no one recognized the movement. Only Gwyn knew that he was riding his wild white horse and trampling out his hatred under its speeding hooves.

The autumn was made of halcyon days.

Warm air and soft winds and bright sunshine.

Gwyn needed high winds.

He longed for the riding gales through which he could gallop endlessly. His horse was changing colour. As his hatred grew, so did the white turn to grey, to dark grey, to black.

It was not yet quite as deep as the midnight sky, but the day that the blackness was absolute, that would be his day.

The weather changed.

A little wind blustered and grew to a big wind, and

that in turn grew to a gale.

It grew to a gale that turned to a tempest. Slates were hurled from roofs; Gryff's little shed, new built, soared over the hedge and crashed to drive the sheep pell mell, bleating in panic.

The cattle stampeded.

Sula, going out to the hens, was almost blown over and ran back to the house, afraid for her baby and her animals. The little seals were now large; but neither of them would take to the sea. When Sula led them to the water they swam happily, but as soon as she left the beach they followed her and once, when Hugh had gone with the fishermen and put them overboard, they followed the boat back and made their own way through the village street and back to the farmhouse.

Now they belonged, with the dogs.

Gwyn took his catapult and took his silver bullets and he took his bomb.

It was a beautiful bomb, a witch bomb, with magic in its depths.

The cover for it was silvery, glinting with light. Inside the dried herbs and plants were powdery, coloured with the colours of verdigris and slime yellow; with witch green and dragon yellow; and into it Gwyn had mixed dried blood from the meat he had killed, and mould from the bread in the bin, and the brilliant scarlet skins of poisonous toadstools.

He had written the best curse he knew.

He cursed Sula and Hugh and the child from day dawn to day dawn, from midnight to moonrise, from May morn to May morn, from darkness to dusk; from dusk to dawn and back again. Some of the words looked strange because he did not know how to spell them.

Hugh found the paper with its spidery letters.

He drew the cross and he prayed by the pool, and

121

he went to the wishing well.

He was thin with worry and the way was easy.

Inside was peace and he wished for more peace.

For an end to fear.

He wished they might catch Gwyn and put him safely away where he could harm no one.

Another thatched roof had burned last night; they put out the fire fast.

No one had seen Gwyn come, and no one saw him go.

He was hidden in the shadows, watching, waiting, looking up at the sky, longing for a wild night, a night when the wind would do his work, would fan the flames.

Long ago his mother had loved fire too.

She had told him of the Great Fire in London, started in Pudding Lane. And she sang to him.

That night when he rose on the mountain he sang that song too.

'London's burning, London's burning.

Fire, fire, fire.'

His horse was blacker than ever before; soon he would be jet black, night black, black as the eternal pit itself.

Gwyn's time would come.

He rode on the wind and shouted with the wind, and his words were flung against the mountain, borne back to him among the wind-noise, the drumming in the trees, the beating of the wild waves against the beaches.

Wind roar.

Wave roar.

Gwyn roar.

He laughed at the moon that was scudding through the sky, tossed among wild clouds like a ship on a wild sea.

Tomorrow would be time.

Tomorrow the wind would strengthen and the waves would pound against the cliffs and the spray toss high, and he would fling his bullets, throw his bomb and burn the village to the ground.

Tomorrow Gwyn would be King upon the mountain.

Gwyn grew reckless that night.

He was seen in the village street, but no one could catch him as he hid in a barn among the hay, burrowing into it like a rat, wild and wicked, with a bomb and bullets instead of sharp, biting teeth.

He lay in the hay while the wind threw itself against the houses and challenged the trees.

He did not want to burn this hay.

It offered him shelter.

It fed his horse.

He looked outside at dusk and saw his horse.

Blacker than midnight, darker than night, a deep shadow among paler shadows.

Now was the time.

He jumped from the stack and galloped down the village street, yelling.

'Heigh, heigh, heigh, heigh.

I'm Gwyn, I'm King, I'm Gwyn come to reign over you.

Heigh, heigh, heigh, heigh.'

The men came from their houses.

Evans the Post and Dai the Police; Hugh and Gryff and Bill who had only just arrived for the weekend; Ianto the Mill and Jones the Vaults, and the old men who sat in the shadows and smoked their pipes and talked of fish bigger than they had ever caught and games faster than they had ever played, and the days when they were young and the world much braver than it was now.

Gwyn threw his bomb.

He would save his bullets till he had time to catch the witch. Maybe she would burn in the fire.

He had put a firelighter in with the herbs, just to make sure.

Such a bomb as men had never seen.

They stared in disbelief as Gwyn tossed it into the sky, the flames from the firelighter burning the herbs, a stench such as no one had smelled before coming from it.

Bill ran and caught it, burning his hands and threw it in the horse trough.

The flames sputtered and died.

Gwyn stared at them from the end of the village street.

They began to move.

They moved slowly, steadily, relentlessly, shoulder to shoulder, as baleful as the incoming tide.

There was nowhere to go but the cliffs.

Thunder rolled on the hills.

Thunder for Gwyn, the voice of his horse, the voice of his fury. He was power, he was magic, he was able to outrun them all.

They came like the marching tide, the destroying waves, shoulder to shoulder, slowly, powerfully and menacingly.

The path across the clifftops was narrow, bordered by high brambles, by heather and by thorn; it was not easy for the black horse, for it was slippery with rain.

It led to the cursing well, Gwyn's favourite place.

Beyond the well were the passages that led to the beach.

There he could escape and he would make another bomb.

He turned and flung his silver bullets from the catapult, both together.

They fell in the heather. The men marched on.

Gwyn reined his horse and kneed his horse and drove his horse forward.

All the men saw was Gwyn, running as if the devil were at his heels, as perhaps he was.

The men moved on, till they came to the cliff path, and then they flowed along it, one man and another man, a solid army of men, a hunting army of men, Dai leading them.

The moon showed through the gaps in the clouds and then it died.

Gwyn galloped on.

On through the heather and on through the bramble, tearing his hands on the thorns.

The thunder rumbled all around him.

Wind tore the clouds from the moon.

The moon shone full on the cliffs, made a path into the sea, and there, when Hugh looked, were the seal heads; hundreds of seals, looking upwards, watching.

The cliffs had fallen on their beach; and they had come for shelter from a wind that they knew would outroar any wind that had ever been, crashing the waves against the shore, tearing the babies from their mothers, dashing small pups against the rocks.

The men saw the massed heads, and stared at them.

Gwyn saw the seals and knew the witch woman had summoned them.

He shook his fist at them, calling spells against them.

He roared with the wind and the thunder.

The wind grew, pushing against the men, pushing against Gwyn.

He knew the witch woman had summoned the wind. It had turned against him.

He called on his horse to carry him to safety.

He called on the wind to turn and destroy the men and the village and the seal woman and her pup.

125

He knew she was down there in the tossing white waters; that somewhere among the beasts was her head; that somewhere among the pups was her pup.

On the hills the sheep hid in the hollows.

The cattle crouched under walls.

The women listened to the wind fearfully.

Sula locked herself in the farmhouse and nursed her baby. Even the dogs trembled, and the seals lay beside her, while she watched the flames and prayed for safety for the men who should not be out on such a wild night.

She remembered the night of the storm and her tiny boat; it seemed so long ago. She had a new life now; a good life, were it not for Gwyn.

The moon had gone.

The men were marching in darkness, but ahead of them they heard Gwyn's voice.

Heigh, heigh, heigh.

He was through the heather and bramble, on the path that led to the cursing well.

Down, down, down, and now lightning flashed in the sky.

Fireflash, flickerflash, lightning flash.

Heigh, heigh, heigh.

The sounds were tossed into the thunder.

Thunder rumbled and rolled and echoed.

The hills shook.

Gwyn reached the well and stood in the lightning flashes that poured over him, as if he were part of the storm. The men stopped, appalled.

They stared down, and the sky was rent in two.

The lightning forks struck again and again at the well, at the rocks around it, and at Gwyn.

The rock split in two.

Gwyn vanished.

Nothing was left but the sound of his voice ringing out with the thunder.

Heigh, heigh, heigh.

He was plunging down, down, into the sea.

Among the seals that would rend him. They heard him scream in terror. And then — nothing.

The men stood together, afraid to move, not knowing where the earth had split, unable to see or hear for the rain was falling. It smashed against them, hailstones crashed against the ground, so that they huddled against one another, lying in the heather, while beyond them, where once had been the cursing well and Hugh's cottage, the ground had opened and swallowed Gwyn up.

The wind dropped.

The rain ceased.

The thunder rumbled softly and at last was only a far away murmur in the hills.

The dawn came.

The men stared.

Only a hundred yards beyond them, the cliff had fallen. The rocks had shivered and slipped. A black chasm yawned in front of them. The cursing well had gone. Where the dark waters had lain sullen under the sun was now another deep crack, that delved into the earth and vanished into the far away darkness.

Beside the crack was a piece of old slate.

Hugh looked at it, and flung it into the sea. His hand tingled when he touched it, as if it held the evil of centuries in its grip.

It hung, black against the blue sky, and dived into the deep waters.

The men watched it go.

Below them the beach was alive with seals, sheltering after the wild night.

The men returned to the village.

Bill looked at Gwyn's bomb; a pathetic bag of rubbish.

He and Hugh and Gryff and Dai took it and buried it deep.

It was an absurd thing, a harmless thing, and yet . . .

Peace returned to the village.

Hugh and Sula stayed with Gryff and their son grew up, never knowing of the past, but down in the village, when thunder rumbled and the wind blew strong and the hills echoed with noises and words that sounded like heigh, heigh, heigh, the children who remembered looked at one another uneasily and stayed indoors in case Gwyn had come for them on his black horse.

THE END